Quinceañera means ♥ sweet 15

Veronica Chambers

SCHOLASTIC INC.

New York Toronto London Auckland Sydney
Mexico City New Delhi Hong Kong Buenos Aires

For Caroline, Erika, Kelly, Sharon, and Lisa
Mejores amigas and phenomenal women
Who opened their circle of friendship and let me in.

And with humble gratitude to
The National Endowment of the Arts
for supporting my writing and to
Terry McMillan for the vote of confidence.
Thank you.

This book is set in Perpetua.

ISBN 0-439-12396-8
(meets NASTA specifications)

5   6   7   8   9   10   23   13 12 11 10 09 08 07 06

1

No money, no *quince*, no dress. I tried to explain this to my best friend, Magdalena Rosario, as we headed toward the bus stop. But the girl had a mind of her own. *"No seas tan negativa,"* Magda said, wagging a finger at me. "We'll figure this out."

"This" being the question of my "Sweet 15" party, or *quinceañera.* The fact was that my mom didn't have the money to throw me a big bash and Magda's family had been saving for her *quince* practically since the day she was born. Magda's sister, Evelyn, had had a huge *quince* the year before. Now it was Magda's turn, and she could hardly wait. Which was why, for the third time in a week, we were on our way to the mall to look at *quince* dresses.

"I don't know why you won't just have a double *quince* with me," Magda said, reaching into her pocket for a MetroCard to pay the busfare.

It was a cool November afternoon in Brooklyn, where we live. I could see the bus ambling toward us and felt a cold wind on my face. It hadn't snowed yet, but it would soon.

"Hello?" Magda said, shaking a head full of wavy jet-black hair in my face. "Am I talking to myself?"

I smiled. "I'm sorry, Magda," I said. "I was thinking about snow."

Magda grimaced as she pulled her puffy pink jacket tighter around her neck.

"Don't even say that word to me!" Magda said. "I bet you didn't miss the snow when you were in Panama."

"*Qué piensas?*" I laughed. "You know I didn't."

A little over a year before, when I was thirteen, I had gone to live with my *abuela*, my grandmother, in Panama, while my mom finished graduate school. At first, I thought I was going to hate it. I'd never met my grandmother before. I'd never even visited Panama. I was born here, in the U.S. of A. I was so afraid of leaving Mami and my best friend, Magda. When Mami first brought up the idea she didn't understand why I was so upset.

"You're going *home*," she would say excitedly.

"*Your* home," I muttered for weeks. "You're the one from Panama, not me."

But though I hated to admit it, Mami *tenía razón*. If

Panama didn't feel like home at first, that quickly changed. I fell in love with Abuela and I made some great friends.

Going away, though, made things pretty funky between me and Magda. Even though I'd been back for almost six months, she still brought up my going to Panama all the time, as if she was afraid that I was going to up and leave her at any given moment.

I'd be lying if I said that Panama hadn't changed me. Before I went away, I pretty much depended on Magda for everything. Her mom and my mom grew up together, and Magda and I had been friends since we were babies. It was like we had no choice but to be best friends. And the thing is, Magda's always been the one in charge. When we were little, she was the one who picked what games we were going to play and made up all the rules.

Magda has this way about her. Whether she's talking to a cute guy, or trying out the latest dance moves, she approaches everything *con mucha fuerza*. She's fearless. But going to Panama, living in a foreign country, learning how to speak Spanish *como una nativa* had given me a sense of confidence that I never had before. In some ways, I had become a little fearless myself.

I can tell that while Magda was glad to have me back, she didn't know quite what to make of the new me. Sometimes, I saw her watching me, studying me, to see how I had changed. I knew that she was looking for something like those scenes in the movies where the quiet, plain librarian takes off her glasses and shakes her hair out of the bun on top of her head and becomes a beautiful siren. But the things that had changed about me were things that couldn't be seen.

Getting dressed for school in the morning, I gazed in the mirror and saw the same chocolate-brown skin, the same curly twists of hair, except now they were shoulder length. I was taller, but I was still skinny, with boobs like distant stars, invisible to the naked eye. I had changed, but the changing hadn't stopped. Tía China, my favorite aunt, said that fifteen was the year that I would become a young woman and would no longer be a *jovencita*. That's why the *quince* is so important. In olden days, when a girl had her *quince*, she could get married! I couldn't imagine being married now or anytime soon. But I knew that a *quince* meant big things were on the way.

I had been waiting my whole life to be fifteen, to be a woman. I knew one birthday doesn't change your life, but a *quince* is different. On your fifteenth birthday, you're surrounded by your family and your friends and they've gathered to say, "You're grown and I see this in you. You're no longer a child and I won't treat you that way."

The bus pulled up and Magda and I took seats near the back. "Six months isn't that long," Magda said, referring to our spring birthdays. Magda was born the end of April. I was born the first of May. "My mom says it really takes a year to plan a proper *quince*."

"I like your eye shadow," I said, admiring the curve of shimmery lavender powder that covered her lids.

Magda smiled, her glossy purple lips turning upward. "Really? Thanks," she said, appreciatively. "You know I'm glad

I didn't go out for drill team this year. I really need all my after-school time to plan for my *quince*."

"I wish there was an art club I could join," I said, opening my notebook to a watercolor that I had done for art appreciation class.

"What do you think?"

Magda took the notebook out of my hand and examined it for a good five minutes, making "hmmm" and "hrrmph" sounds throughout.

"Well, it looks a lot like a bowl of plums," she said. I grabbed the notebook back and laughed.

"Way to go, Sherlock," I said. "I was asking you whether or not it was a good picture."

She shrugged. "It's *fine*. You've always been good at art. *Muévete*, this is our stop."

In the Junior Formal department, we tried on one dress after another. We could only take three dresses at a time into the dressing room, so we ran around like madwomen grabbing from the racks. Magda tried on a gorgeous midnight-blue dress with a fur collar.

"*Bonita, no?*" Magda asked, hopefully.

I nodded my head yes. "But it's too Russian princess-y. You need a dress with more flavor."

Magda came out with a purple dress with a big bow in the back. She threw her hands up in the air like a movie star.

"No way," I said. "Too Goody Two-shoes."

"Why don't you try on some dresses?" Magda asked.

I rubbed my fingers together, the way our moms always

do when they're talking about cash. "No dough-re-mi," I explained.

Magda just shrugged. "Whatever."

She tried on a blue dress with sequins, a pink dress with sequins, and a light green dress with sheer-illusion sleeves; it looked like the same kind of dress those champion ice-skater girls wear during the Winter Olympics. I wished there were an Olympic competiton for most exhaustive window shopping, 'cause Magda and I would win first place for sure.

For the umpteenth time, Magda tried on this long black spandex-y dress with a strapless pearl bodice. It looked great on her. As the guys at our school say, her hips were bumpin'. But Magda's mom was so religious. Even if she let the clingy fabric slide, there was absolutely no way she was going to let Magda wear black for her *quince*. She could hardly stand the way Magda dressed already. *"Pero, niña,"* she always said when she saw Magda in head-to-toe black. "You know black is for funerals."

I wandered over to the other side of the store floor while Magda got dressed. There were so many beautiful dresses. My fingers instinctively reached for each price tag, then I quickly looked away and moved on. Then I saw a dress on a mannequin that I couldn't stop staring at. It was cranberry red, floor length, with spaghetti straps and a sheer-illusion waist.

"It's like an Oscar dress," Magda said, approvingly.

I jumped at the sound of her voice. "I didn't see you there," I said. *"Bellísima, no?"*

Magda jumped up on the box with the mannequin and threw both her arms in the air and posed. "I just want to thank all the little people. . . ." she said, in a fab British accent. Magda was great at accents. I just rolled my eyes.

"You'll have to step down," said a young saleswoman. She was about twenty-five, dressed in a black pantsuit and funky retro tortoiseshell eyeglasses.

"Would you like to try the dress on?" the saleswoman asked.

"Not me, my friend," Magda said, climbing down.

"What size?" the saleswoman asked me. I felt a little nervous then. I kept thinking that maybe I shouldn't be trying on dresses I had no money to buy.

"Size seven," I squeaked.

The saleswoman went to get the dress and I grabbed Magda by the sleeve.

"What am I *doing*?" I asked. "I can't afford this dress. I don't even know if I'm going to have a *quince*."

"It doesn't hurt to try it on," Magda said. *"No te preocupes."*

I took the dress from the saleswoman and entered the dressing room, pulling the velvet blue curtain closed. I undressed and stared for a second at my reflection in the mirror. I always thought the same thing about my skinny legs and puny breasts. Everything in the teen magazines was about how most girls want to be thin—some even starved themselves to do it. But in our neighborhood, guys seemed to like girls with round breasts and curves. "Can I get some fries to go with that shake?" they'd call out to my Tía China when we walked down the street. As much as it embarrassed me, there was a part of me that wanted them to call out the same things to me.

"Come on, *niña*," Magda called into the dressing room. "Today, not tomorrow."

I stepped from behind the curtain and self-consciously straightened the skirt of the dress.

"What do you think?" I asked.

"Amazing," Magda said. "You should buy it right now."

I felt my chest tighten and willed myself not to cry. Magda knew I didn't have the money to buy the dress. Sometimes it was like she said careless things on purpose.

"That dress is so beautiful on you," echoed the salesgirl, whose name tag said ANN. She straightened one of the straps while I admired myself in the mirror.

"You're so tall, you can pull off wearing so much red," Ann said. "Not to mention that it looks beautiful against your skin."

I agreed, pausing to turn and admire myself in the mirror. I held my hair back and imagined the *quince* crown on my head.

"It's perfect," Magda whispered.

I tiptoed back to the dressing room on the balls of my feet, as if I were wearing a pair of stylish high heels. Then as I took the dress off, I looked at the price tag again. The dress was beautiful, but it sure wasn't a bargain. It costs hundreds. Even if Mami could swing it, there was no way she could come up with the money for the dress *and* a proper *quince*.

Magda poked her head into the dressing room. "Stop day-dreaming, Mayaguez," she said, giving me a shake.

"Okay, I'm coming," I said, pulling the dressing room curtain closed. "Some privacy, puh-leeze?"

I snuggled back into my turtleneck and jeans, feeling a lot like Cinderella five minutes after midnight. I looked at the cranberry formal dress, hanging like a dream on the hanger before me. I didn't mean to be a snob, but how could I wear a dress like that to a party in Tía Alicia's basement? *Fíjese.* No way. No how.

I handed the dress back to the saleswoman. "Not today, thank you," I said.

"Good luck," she said, whisking the dream of a dress back toward the rack where it had come from.

Wistfully, I watched her walk away. It was the perfect dress.

"What you thinking 'bout?" Magda asked, playfully.

"I was just thinking about how in my dreams, my *quince* dress doesn't cost a thing," I explained.

"Let's go," I said, looking at my watch. "It's five-thirty. I better get back home and make dinner for my mom."

"That's cool. I need to pick my little brother up from the day-care center anyway."

We walked out to the bus stop. The wind seemed to whip right through my pea coat. I pulled on my gloves and thought about my beautiful cranberry-red *quinceañera* dress; that was *my* dress.

"Marisol, you know, if you saved up all your baby-sitting

money, you could get that dress," Magda said, as we made our way to the only two empty seats on the bus.

"I was thinking the same thing," I said, putting my knapsack on the floor between my legs. "Maybe I could get another job."

"Mrs. Trader next door is looking for somebody to walk her dog in the evenings," Magda offered.

An image of Tyson, Mrs. Trader's great big German shepherd, flashed through my mind.

"I don't know about *that*."

"Oh, Tyson's not so bad. Besides, I think she's paying ten dollars a pop."

"Well," I said, adding up the money in my head. "That would be sixty dollars a week if she wanted him walked on Saturdays. Hmmm . . . Why is she paying so much?"

"You get extra pay because you've got to clean up behind him," Magda explained.

"Oh, I see. . . . It's not ten dollars a *pop*, it's ten dollars a *poop*."

"*Exactly,*" Magda said, laughing. "But you would have that dress in no time."

She was right. The dress, expensive as it was, was starting to look doable. Now I just needed a *quince* to go with it.

2

I walked through the front door of our apartment and was surprised to see that Mami was already home.

"*Hola, Mami,*" I said, giving her a kiss on the cheek.

"*Hola, loca,*" Mami said, using her new favorite nickname for me. I was hardly crazy, which is what *loca* means, but Mami insisted it fit. "You know how teenagers are today," she would tell her friends. "*Son locos.*"

Since I'd come back from Panama, Mami had finished her master's degree in hospital administration and had gotten a promotion at her job. We had moved out of the apartment that I'd grown up in and were now renting the top floor of a two-family house, not too far from Magda's. It was nice.

There was even a garden. The big magnolia tree in the front made me think of that book, *A Tree Grows in Brooklyn*. But I missed our old place sometimes. I missed Olveen Ortega, the old man from Panama who lived on the first floor. Even if he was just sitting on the front step, Mr. Ortega always dressed in a starched cream-colored shirt and nicely pressed pants with a Panama hat. Sometimes when Mami made *una comida nacional* like *bacalao* with rice, she would give me a plate to take down to Mr. Ortega.

When I went to Panama, I had this whole plan that maybe I'd find my father, whom I've never met. He took off when I was a baby and hasn't been seen since. Mami had all kinds of terrible things to say about my *papi*, that he wasn't responsible, that he didn't like family life. But the fact that I was born and a year later he was history doesn't make me feel really good. I went looking for him in Panama. The first time I went to the apartment, I found his brother, Oscar, who was living there. The second and third time, I left letters with my *abuela*'s address and phone number, hoping that he'd get them when Oscar forwarded his mail. But I never heard anything. I just *knew* that I couldn't come all the way from the United States and live in the same country with him—a country only as big as Pennsylvania—and not find him. But I guess it just goes to show. There's not a thing you can do when somebody doesn't want to be found.

"Come on, help me set the table," Mami said. "Wash your hands first."

I went over to the sink and started to sing, *"Ay, Mamá Inez.*

Todos los negros tomamos café." It was an old folk song that always made Mami laugh because her name was Inez, too.

"*Ay, Mamá Inez,*" I sang once more.

"You're in a good mood. Where were you this afternoon?"

I helped myself to a large serving of lasagna. "The mall. With Magda."

"Let me guess. You were looking at *quince* dresses."

"Bingo."

"See anything you like?" Mami asked. Her short curly hair was slicked back with gel. It was a good style for her.

"I saw a dress that I *loved*. *Era bellísima*. It's a beautiful cherry red. No, it's more like cranberry red—"

Mami put her hand up and signaled, stop. "How much?" she asked.

"A lot," I mumbled.

"How much? I didn't hear you." Mami asked again, opening a can of diet soda.

"Two hundred dollars," I said, swallowing hard.

"Eeech," Mami said as if she'd just found a spider in her food.

"I love it, Mami," I said, taking her hand in mine. "I was thinking I could get another job."

Mami jumped out of her chair and put her hands on her hips. "Are you kidding? Your job, in case you forgot, is to be a good student!" The one thing that made Mami furious was anyone not taking school seriously. "You're already baby-sitting on Saturday nights for the Morales family. Unless you've forgotten, you're going to need a scholarship for college. They don't give those out because you're cute."

"There's always the Miss America pageant," I joked.

Mami tickled the bottom of my chin. "I think you're the most beautiful girl in the world," she said, smiling. "But I'd hate to rest your whole entire college education on a beauty pageant."

"So would I," I agreed. "Magda said that old Mrs. Trader is looking for someone to walk her dog in the evening."

"It's getting dark earlier, you know. I don't know if I like the idea of you walking some dog in the dark."

"Mami, *please.* You see how big Tyson is?"

"You've got a point," she said, giggling. "That's one big dog. You can talk to Mrs. Trader and I'll think about it."

Then she reached out to give a little tug to my twists. "You know I'd give you a *quince* and a dress and the works if I could, Marisol-Mariposa."

"I know," I said softly, as I squeezed her hand.

That night, I felt terrible guilt about putting the whole bother and expense of a *quinceañera* on Mami. I looked around my powder-blue bedroom, which Mami had painted herself. Everything in the room was a reminder of how hard Mami had worked to give me everything I wanted. If a *quinceañera* was out of the question, I should just stop wanting one. But I couldn't stop the wanting. No matter how hard I tried.

3

I stood in front of the Rite Aid pharmacy waiting for Magda, who, as usual, was late. Now that we were in high school, we had to take the subway to school. I didn't mind. I loved standing on the platform with all the grown-ups going to work and hearing the loud screech and burst of air as the train pulled into the station. The bad thing was that if we were late, there was no way to make up for lost time. And Magda was almost always late.

I looked at my watch: seven-forty-five. I'd give her ten more minutes, then I was ghost.

I had just started to walk toward the subway station when I felt an arm on my shoulder.

"Hey, I know you weren't about to leave me," Magda said, breathing heavily and peeling off a pair of beautiful suede gloves. She pulled a MetroCard out of her back pocket, then held it in her teeth as she put her gloves back on.

"Of course I was going to leave. You, my dear, are late," I said in my best schoolteacher voice.

"See, Marisol," she said, sucking her teeth and goose-necking with attitude. "Why do you have to be like that?"

"Like what? Like on time?"

When the train arrived, we rushed for the corner seats, opposite the conductor. A couple of older women gave us dirty looks as we squeezed past them.

"You know we should let the grown-ups sit, right?" I whispered to Magda.

"You are a *total* bore," she whispered.

"Would you like to sit down?" I asked the two women standing before us. I stood and tugged Magda up by her jacket. The two women smiled and took our seats. One of the women had a short Afro like my *mami*'s; I wondered if she had a daughter like me somewhere. I looked down and saw that both of the women wore sneakers and carried their high-heeled shoes in little bags.

I nodded toward their bag and whispered, "They remind me of my *mami*. Always on her feet."

"Yeah, yeah," Magda said, looking around the train car for an empty seat.

"Good luck," I said. "This train is packed. Of course, if you'd been on time . . ."

Magda just gave me a look, then smiled broadly. "Bingo," she said. "There goes Javier Avril. He better give me his seat."

I followed her through the train, her pink jacket flashing in and out of the gray, brown, and black suits all around us. When I caught up to her, she had zoned in on Javier for one of her flirting games.

"Yo, Marisol," Javier said. "What's up?" Back in fifth grade, Javier and I had played Dungeons and Dragons. I was the only girl who played, and ever since then, Javier had always been really nice to me.

"Come on, Javier," Magda said. "Let me sit down. I'm so tired."

Javier was sitting with two of his homeboys, Jeff and Kendall. Jeff jumped to his feet.

Jeff was this tall, skinny Jamaican dude who lived down the block from our old apartment building. He'd had a crush on Magda forever.

"You can have my seat, Magda," he said. "Lovely as you look today, mon. I'd be happy to stand."

"Thank you, Jeff," Magda said, sweetly. "But the seat I really want is Javier's."

Javier focused intensely on the video game in his hand. He expertly maneuvered the weapons of the game with his chubby fingers, paying Magda no mind. I knew then she was going to make a scene until he paid her some attention.

"This hand has a mind of its own," Magda said, waving five long red fingernails in Javier's face. "If I hit you, it's not my fault."

"Oh shoot," Kendall said, laughing. "She's threatening you, man."

"It's not a threat," Magda said, turning on the charm. "I mean I went to the doctor and he said that my left hand was uncontrollable. It has something to do with my nervous system. So if I just happen to hit you in the face . . ."

She moved her hand quickly toward his face and then touched him lightly on the cheek. She puckered her red lips, leaned in, and kissed Javier right on the lips.

Jeff and Kendall started to make cat noises. "Way to go!" they hooted, punching Javier on the arm and mussing up his air.

"Go ahead, take the seat," Javier said, finally. He looked embarrassed, but pleased. "It's only one more stop."

"Thank you, Javier," Magda said. "Hey, Marisol, let me hold your books."

I gave them to her and shook my head. Magda sure knew how to get her way. She just looked up at me and winked.

When the train pulled into 23rd Street, the boys raced off, but Magda and I hung back, stopping to window shop at Loehmann's and Barnes and Noble.

"You are amazing," I said.

"What do you mean?" Magda asked, in the fake innocent voice she usually reserved for teachers and parents.

"The way you flirted with Javier. *Pobrecito*," I said as we climbed the stairs out of the subway. "The sad part is, you don't even like him."

"Just 'cause I don't like him doesn't mean I shouldn't flirt with him. You know, practice makes perfect," Magda said, reapplying her lipstick in the reflection of the store window.

"I guess so," I said as we headed toward Chavez High School. I looked at my watch: eight-forty-five. We would just make the bell. We were lucky we had Mrs. Butcher for homeroom and that she wasn't that strict about late passes.

After the last bell, Magda was waiting for me by my locker.

"*Qué pasa, loca?*" she asked, grinning at me.

"Not much," I said. "Can I come over to your house after school?"

"Of course, let's go," she said, hooking my arm into hers. We were skipping down the hallway the way we had in kindergarten when someone called out, "Yo, Magda, wait up."

It was Marisa, with a girl named Elizabeth tagging along behind her. Magda chilled with them when I was in Panama the year before. Now that I was home, Magda and I were back to being *mejores amigas*, but she was still cool with Marisa and Elizabeth. Marisa was a short Puerto Rican girl with light brown ringlets and beautiful full lips. Elizabeth was Marisa's best friend, and as far as I could see, her personal servant. She was kind of chubby with hair the color of candy apples and a shy, nervous smile. I guess I was jealous of them, Marisa especially. But the bottom line was, I didn't like them and they didn't like me.

"*Hola, 'manita,*" Marisa said, giving Magda a kiss on the

cheek. She was *always* trying to act like she was so grown. Who do you know in high school who kisses their friends hello?

"Hey, Marisol," Elizabeth said shyly.

"Marisol," Marisa said, sniffing in my direction.

Marisa was wearing an outfit right out of the pages of a fashion magazine: designer jeans, an expensive leather jacket, and beautiful gold hoop earrings. I could tell by the weight and shine of the earrings that they weren't *fantasía*, or fake gold. Those babies were real.

"Nice earrings," I said, admiringly. "Are they new?"

"Do they look old?" Marisa said snippily.

It wasn't really funny, but Elizabeth snickered anyway.

"We're going shop-ping," Marisa said, dragging out the words. "Magda, are you coming?"

"What do you think, Marisol?" Magda asked, pulling my sleeve. "It'll be fun."

"I'll pass," I said.

"We'll live," Marisa said in a snooty tone. Then she, Elizabeth, and my so-called best friend walked away. Now what was that about?

4

The next day, after school, Marisa and Elizabeth were waiting with Magda at my locker. Were they always going to be around? What was the deal?

"Hey," I said, as calmly as I could. "What's up?"

"We're going shopping," Magda explained.

"Again?" I asked.

"We're going to look at *quince* dresses," Elizabeth said, dreamily. "I can hardly wait until my *quince*."

"Marisol found the most beautiful dress at the mall the other day," Magda said. "Tell them about it."

I looked at Marisa and Elizabeth, doubting that they wanted to hear about my dress.

"Come on," Magda said, tugging my sleeve. "Tell them about it."

"Okay," I said smiling. "It's cranberry red, with spaghetti straps and a sheer-illusion waist."

"And does it have a sheer-illusion price tag? 'Cause I'm wondering how you're going to pay for it." Marisa said, guffawing. "They won't take food stamps to pay for a *quinceañera* dress, I'll tell you now."

I felt my face get hot with embarrassment and for a second, I thought I might throw up.

"Okay, Marisa, that's enough," Magda said, quietly.

"I am not on welfare!" I looked around nervously, but there was no one in the hall but us.

"That's not what Magda told me," Marisa said, flipping her curly hair over her shoulder.

"What?" I whispered.

"When you were in Panama, Magda told us all about you, Cinderella," Marisa hissed. "You can't afford a *quince*, then *olvídale*. Go to McDonald's and celebrate with a Happy Meal. Or better yet, go to Burger King. At least there, you'd get a crown."

"What—did—you—tell—them—about me?" I stammered in Magda's direction.

"I was just saying that you didn't have much loot," Magda said, plaintively. "I didn't mean no harm."

I slipped on my jacket, opened the front door, and ran as fast as I could toward the subway. I thought I heard Magda call me, but I was too afraid to turn around and look. The sidewalks were so full of people, I felt like I was running an obstacle course. I swerved to the left to avoid hitting an Indian woman pushing her baby in a stroller. I could see the blue-and-gold print of her sari beneath her black wool coat. I mumbled "Excuse me," as I tried to squeeze past a group of businessmen carrying briefcases and laptop computers. I stopped short behind an old woman who was walking so slowly I thought I would scream. But finally, I reached the subway station.

I bounded down the steps, taking them two at a time. I fished around in my pocket for my MetroCard. I swiped it once, but it didn't go through. "Damn it," I groaned at the green neon readout that said SWIPE AGAIN. I did; the card clicked. I pushed the turntile and rushed down the steps again. On the platform, I stopped, finally, to catch my breath. I pulled my navy pea coat closer to me. The coat had belonged to Tía China; half the things I owned had belonged to someone else. I loved my coat—or at least, I *had* loved it before Marisa ripped on it.

This is what it's like to feel poor, I realized. You look at everything you have and nothing is good enough. You look in the mirror and you feel that *you're* not good enough. Before all the *quinceañera* drama, I had never really thought that much about money. I knew we had less money than Magda's family, but I figured that was because she had a dad and I didn't. I knew that Mami made me wear a lot of hand-me-down clothes, but I thought that was because we were Panamanian and never wasted anything. "*Es como nuevo para ti,*"

Mami would say cheerfully, as she gave me sweaters and scarves that the *tías* would drop off.

The concrete platform was teeming with life—people talking and laughing and arguing. Near the stairs, a man with a trumpet played a jazz song. The trumpet case in front of him lay open, with shiny coins glittering like diamonds against the black velvet lining. Poor people were people like that guy, I thought. People who asked for money on the street. Not me, I thought. Not me.

Just then the train arrived with a gust of wind like God trying to blow out a birthday candle. I walked into the car when I heard someone call my name.

"Marisol," Magda cried out. "Wait up."

I could see her at the top of the steps. If I held the door for her, she could make it. But there was no way. No way in hell. I stepped into the car and the doors closed behind me. As the train pulled away, I could see her on the platform, getting smaller in the distance. And then she was gone.

5

It was Saturday afternoon. I sat at the kitchen table, cutting out pictures from magazines for my *quince* dream notebook. There were so many little things to think about. The dress. The banquet hall. The music. But that was just stuff, there was the whole *quince* ceremony. I knew I wouldn't be able to afford a full *quinceañera* court with fifteen *damas*, most likely I'd have seven *damas*, as Ana Marie had. Who would my seven *damas* be? Magda was number one on my list. Though not if she kept playing me like a trick deck of cards. But who else? I didn't have that many friends. It was days like this that I missed my best friend from Panama, Ana.

I cut out a picture of a girl in a pretty lavender dress.

I glued it into my notebook of dreams. If I ended up wearing white, lavender would be a pretty color for my *damas*. What about my date? Who would be my special *caballero*? Would my *quince* have a theme? Mami always called me Marisol-Mariposa. Maybe I could use butterflies as my theme. . . . If I had a *quince* at all.

It's tradition, in a *quince*, to give out a souvenir at the end. I knew those would cost a fortune. Most people gave out tiny *capas*, little hats with a ribbon saying the *quince's* name and birthday. Ana Marie had given us all heart-shaped magnets with that said ANA MARIE ARROYO'S QUINCEAÑERA with the date stamped at the bottom. Magda had thrown hers away. "Ugh, tacky," she had said. But I thought it was cute. Mami and I still had the magnet on the fridge.

The doorbell rang. I didn't move from the table.

The doorbell rang twice in long succession. That was Magda's impatient ring. She rang again.

Mami came out of her bedroom and gave me a strange look.

"*Qué te pasa*, Marisol? You don't hear the bell."

She pressed the intercom and asked, "*Quién es?*"

"It's Magda, Señora Mayaguez."

Mami buzzed her in.

She stood over my chair and massaged my left shoulder.

"You and Magda are fighting?"

"Sort of," I whispered.

"Well, make up," Mami said cheerfully, opening the front door.

"*Buenos días*, Señora Mayaguez."

"How are you, Magda?"

"Good, good. What's up, Marisol?"

I didn't say anything.

"I'll leave you girls," Mami said, going back into her room.

Magda sat down at the table. She was wearing designer jeans and a red turtleneck sweater. A pair of gold earrings glistened in her ears.

"I didn't ask you to sit," I growled.

"Come on, Marisol. Don't be like that."

She ran her fingers along my *quince* dream book.

"It's been ages since I wrote in mine," she said. "We should work on ours together."

I knew she was trying to make conversation, but I wasn't in the mood.

"How could you diss me like that to Marisa and Elizabeth?" I asked, my voice getting higher with each word. "How could you make fun of me behind my back?"

"I didn't mean to," Magda said. Her eyes shifted all around the room and her bottom lip quivered the way it did whenever she was in trouble. "I guess I was mad at you for going away. I said all kinds of things I didn't mean."

"Oh yeah? All kinds of things? What other things?"

"I don't know what I said exactly."

"I bet Marisa knows. Maybe I should ask her."

"I know you don't like her," Magda said. "But I had to make friends while you were away."

"Well, I'm back."

"I know and I'm so glad. Don't be mad at me, okay?" Marisol reached into her turtleneck and pulled out the gold cross we had both received from her father at our confirmation.

"*Somos mejores amigas,*" Magda said. "We're best friends. Even God knows that."

"Maybe you need a best friend who has enough money to roll like you do," I said. "Maybe now that we're older I can't afford to be your *mejor amiga.*"

Magda just rolled her eyes. "Come on Marisol. Don't be like that."

"I've got to baby-sit tonight," I said, looking at my watch.

"Okay," she said. "Call me later?"

I nodded, then looked at my watch again.

Magda started to walk away, then paused in the hallway and turned around to give me a hug. I hugged her back.

"*Te hablo,*" I said as she walked down the hall.

"*Te amo,* Marisol," she said as she entered the elevator.

"Yeah?" I wondered aloud as I walked back to my apartment. "You sure have a funny way of showing it."

Mami opened the door of the apartment for me. She looked concerned, but didn't say anything. Mami was good that way.

"I'm going to listen to some music, okay?" I asked.

"*Claro,*" Mami said.

I scanned the rack of CDs and decided on one of Mami's Gloria Estefan albums. "Come on baby, shake your body, do that conga. . . ." I hummed as I walked back into the dining room. No matter what was wrong, Gloria always cheered me up. I sat back at the table and flipped through a magazine without reading a single word. Magda and I had had little fights before, but this one felt bigger. I kept trying to figure out what it was. I knew part of it was that I couldn't stand Marisa, but there was something else. Finally, I hit on it. This was the first time, in a whole lifetime of being best friends that I had felt truly betrayed by Magda. I was glad she had come over. I was glad we had made up. But I never before could have imagined her talking about me behind my back—and now, I knew for a fact, that she had. Just the thought of it made me wince.

Mami sat down at the table and slid a cup of hot chocolate across to me.

"Marshmallows," I said, looking into the cup.

Mami jumped up. "I forgot!"

"*Gracias,* Mami," I said, giving her a *besito* on the cheek.

"*Qué pasa* with you and Magda?" she asked. "Everything okay?"

"Yeah," I said, glumly.

"Doesn't sound like it. Want to talk about it?"

I shook my head no.

"Can I look?" Mami asked, gesturing to my *quince* dream book.

Even though she'd seen me work on it, I'd never actually shown it to her before. I didn't want Mami to feel that I was pushing for a *quince* beyond our means.

"Sure," I said, handing her the notebook. My hand shook slightly as I did. Showing Mami my *quince* dream book was almost as personal as letting her read my diary.

Mami sat back in her chair. In her overalls and turtleneck, she looked as young as Tía China. She opened the page of my dream book and gazed at each page. She turned the notebook sometimes to read the scribbles I'd written down the side of the page. I sat next to her while she went through each section: dresses, handbags, shoes, cakes, napkins, souvenirs, inspirational sayings. In charcoal, I had done sketches of all the people that I loved. I had drawn Mami, with her short hair and sharp cheekbones.

"That really looks like me!" Mami said. "*De veras*, it looks prettier than me."

On the following page, I had drawn Papi from the one photo I had of him when he and Mami were teenagers. I had spent hours trying to perfectly achieve his mere shadow of a beard. I had cried when I drew his dark eyes with eyelashes that seemed too long, too beautiful for a man. It had been hard, too, to draw his smile, wondering what were the sounds beneath the broad, white teeth. What did it sound like when my *papi* laughed? Did he chuckle, in a deep baritone, like Tío Diego? Or did he laugh, mouth wide open, like my *novio* Rubén had? These were the kind of questions Mami never wanted to answer.

Mami stared at the picture of Papi for what seemed like an eternity. Then she flipped the page.

"What do you think?" I asked, turning the page back to Papi's image.

"It looks just like him," Mami whispered, her hand rubbing the small of my back. "You're a very good artist."

Mami smiled at my drawing of Abuela and exclaimed at how well I'd managed to capture the likenesses of Magda, Tía China, Ana, and Rubén. On the last page, she paused. I'd drawn a picture of myself in a white Cinderella dress. In the picture, I wore white gloves and a diamond tiara. It was the first self-portrait I'd ever done. It drove me crazy to stare at myself so long in the mirror, but it was important for me to do the drawing. If I wasn't going to be able to be a *quinceañera* in real life, at least I'd get to be one on the page.

"This is beautiful. I ought to frame it," Mami said. "You will make a beautiful *quinceañera*."

She hugged me then. "My daughter, the artist," she said, playfully flopping a handful of my twists with her hand.

I sat down, cross-legged on the dining room chair. Mami sat next to me and stretched her legs across another chair. Then she opened the book again. In purple pen ink, on the last page, I'd taped a *quince* card with a poem that inspired me:

"Hoy, es el día de tu quince,
has esperándole por tanto tiempo.
Hoy, todos los estrellas se brillan
y empiezas un destino nuevo.
Tu familia y todos tus amigos,
juntaron por celebrar este día.
Todavia no eres una niña,
ahora, eres una señorita.

En este día, te cumples quince años,
hay un mundo entiro por descubrir.
un mundo de possibilidades,
un mundo de oportunidades,
esperando solamente por tú a aprovechar!

Today is your fifteenth birthday;
you've waited for this for so long.
Today, the stars shine upon you
and you begin a new path.
Your family and your friends
have gathered to celebrate this day.
You are no longer a little girl;
today, you are a young woman.
On this day, you turn fifteen years old;
there's a whole world for you to discover.
A world of possibilities,
A world of opportunities,
just waiting for you to reach out and grab them!

Mami read the poem aloud in Spanish, then I read it in English. She closed the book and said, "You know I never had a *quince*. Neither did your *tías*, Julia and Alicia. The only reason China was able to have a *quince* was that we were all older and working so we could help out. Still, it was cheaper 'cause China had her *quince* in Panama. Here, *todo es demasiado caro*, very expensive."

Mami stood up from the table and nodded toward the

kitchen. "*Ven.* I've got to soak the peas for Sunday's dinner," she said. Every Sunday, Mami made a big dinner: rice and peas cooked in coconut water, curry chicken, potato salad. Hmmm, *sabroso.*

I grabbed our hot-chocolate mugs and sat on top of the washing machine while Mami rinsed the peas at the sink.

"What do you think of this?" Mami said, turning toward me. "We could have your *quince* in Tía Alicia's basement. It's not fancy, but it would be cheap."

"I'd rather not," I said. "We have *all* our parties in Tía Alicia's basement."

"I know, but we could get special *quince* decorations, maybe hire a DJ. It wouldn't feel like a basement party."

"Of course it would. *Tú sabes, Mami*," I whined. "My *quince* is supposed to be special."

"Unfortunately, *hija*, your definition of special is also expensive," she sighed heavily in the way she always did when she talked about money or our lack of it. "You know I didn't even have a *quince*."

"I know, Mami," I said, feeling guilty.

"I want to give you the world, Marisol-Mariposa."

"You already have, Mami. Look at our new apartment. The kitchen is like new! There's no elevator with graffiti or guys hanging outside. We have a *garden*. I never thought we'd have a garden."

"I'm glad you like it, *cariña*. When I sent you to Panama to live with your *abuela* so I could finish school, I was worried that I was doing the wrong thing. You should have seen your little face at the airport! As you walked away from me, you looked as if you were being sent to your doom."

I was embarrassed. "But I didn't know how much I would like Panama!"

"How could you not have liked it? It's our home, our *patria*."

"Your homeland, Mami. *Soy americana.* I'm American."

"I'm American, too." Mami grinned. "Central American."

"Whatever!" I said, making a W with my thumbs and forefingers.

"By the way, I have a date tonight," Mami said. She smiled and her voice rose the way it always did when she was excited. "I'll drop you off to baby-sit Kiki, and I'll be home by the time the Moraleses bring you home."

I sat there, stunned.

"A date? With who?" It had been so long since Mami had been out with any guy. I don't know, I figured maybe she'd given up on the whole thing.

"His name is Eduardo Navarro. He's an X-ray technician at the hospital."

"Do you like him?"

"I wouldn't be going out on a date with him if I didn't."

"Where are you going?"

"What is this, twenty questions?"

"I've got *at least* twenty questions."

"Hey, *cálmate*," Mami said, putting one hand on her hip. "Don't forget who's the mother and who's the child."

"I'm just curious, that's all."

"How'd you meet him?"

"I've known him for years. Then last year, he got divorced from his wife and we started to talk more. We eat lunch together all the time, but this will be our first real date."

Divorced? Maybe, I thought, this guy has kids. I had always wanted a brother or sister, preferably a sister.

"Does he have kids?"

"No," Mami says. "He would like to, though."

"With who? You?"

"I'm not so old!" Mami exclaimed. "I could still have kids." Mami looked away for a second and put her hand on her stomach.

I puffed out my cheeks and stuck out my stomach as if I were pregnant. "Mami, no. You're so pretty now. I'd hate to see you become a human blimp!"

Mami just rolled her eyes. "Let's not rush things, this is just our first date. *No debes planear todo nuestra vida.*"

"What are you going to wear?"

"Clothes."

And on that note, she disappeared into her bedroom.

6

When Mami emerged from her bedroom, all dressed up for her date, I was way impressed. She was wearing a gold-colored jacket with her good gold earrings (the ones she had brought with her from Panama), and a long black skirt. She was also wearing a pair of gold-colored high heels that I'd never seen before.

"New shoes?" I asked. "Nice. You look so fancy, like you're going to a ball."

Mami looked panicked. "Is it too much?" she asked, rushing over to the hallway mirror. "I don't want to overdo it."

"Welllllll," I said. "I don't want to ask any more questions 'cause I know you don't like them. But where are you going?"

"Eduardo's made dinner reservations at a really nice restaurant in the city. It's called Calle Ocho. They serve Cuban food."

"Well, you look really good."

"I hope so," Mami said, nervously fussing in the hallway mirror.

"Why are you so nervous, Mami? *Eres bella.* Is this guy a super-hunk or something?"

Mami laughed. "No, I wouldn't exactly call Eduardo a super-hunk. . . ."

Just then the bell rang.

"Speak of the devil. I'll get it." I jumped up and pressed the button for the intercom. "Who is it?"

A deep voice answered, "*Soy yo*, Eduardo."

"Eduardo who?" I answered.

"Eduardo Navarro," the voice answered.

"Are you the pizza delivery boy? We didn't order any pizza."

All I heard over the intercom was a weird laugh. "Heh, heh, heh."

Mami turned around and pinched me. "*Basta.* Stop playing around."

"Okay, okay," I said, buzzing Eduardo in.

Mami spritzed herself with Carolina Herrera perfume and carefully applied a layer of deep-red lipstick. I noticed she had also painted her nails red. Mami always wore clear polish. She said hospital work was too messy for anything else.

"You look fantastic," I said again. It was strange watching Mami get ready for a date. But it was double strange to see her be so nervous.

The doorbell to our apartment rang and Mami opened it. All I heard was a whistle and then a "*Mírale*, Mami!"

Eduardo Navarro walked into our apartment and reached out to shake my hand. He was fair-skinned and tall, with wavy dark hair and a thin mustache. You could see he had been cute, once. But now he was sort of heavy and looked more like a *papi* than a *papi chulo*, which is what me and Magda called cute guys.

"So nice to meet you, Marisolita."

I grimaced and shook his hand back. *Nobody* called me Marisolita.

"My name is Marisol," I said.

"That's what I said. I know your name," Eduardo said, adjusting his suit jacket around his round stomach.

"You called me Marisolita."

"Same thing."

"No, it's not."

"In Puerto Rico, adding an *ito* or an *ita* is our way of making a nickname," Eduardo said. "Carlos becomes Carlito. Lupe becomes Lupita. It's a sign of affection."

"A sign of affection? You don't even know me!" How dare he? This guy was truly getting on my nerves.

Mami stepped between us and took each of our hands. "*Ya, basta.* Let's get going. We don't want to be late for dinner."

Mami and I got our coats and we walked over to the elevator. As we rode down to the first floor, Eduardo turned to me.

"I know I don't know you, Marisol," he said. "But I'm really looking forward to getting to know you."

Mami smiled approvingly at him. I just nodded.

After Mami and Eduardo had dropped me off at the Moraleses' and left for their date, I sat Kiki down with a coloring book and a box of crayons and called Magda on the phone.

"You'll never believe this. . . ." I started.

"Your Mami is out on a date with some nerd named Eduardo."

"How'd you know?"

"Come on, now. You know your *mami* tells my *mami* everything."

"*Yo se.* So what do you think?"

"Of what? The nerd? No biggie."

"He called me Marisolita!"

"He's an X-ray technician, Marisol. Think about all the ultra-violet rays his brain has sucked up over the years. He's bound to say stupid things."

I laughed. "I don't think you get ultraviolet rays from an X-ray machine."

"Marisol, I'm hungry," Kiki said, tugging on my jeans leg. "Make me a sandwich."

I held the phone away from my ear. "Make me a sandwich, *please*," I said.

"Please, make me a sandwich, please," Kiki said, sweetly.

I bent down and gave her a kiss on the cheek. "In two minutes, okay?

"I've got to bounce, Magda."

"Okay, see you tomorrow," she said.

"Cool."

By the time Mrs. Morales drove me home, it was after midnight. I let myself into our apartment and found Mami at the table, sitting in her robe and sipping a *cafecito*.

"*Hola, preciosa,*" Mami said. "Do you want a cup of tea? Hot chocolate?"

"I'm good," I said, taking off my coat and joining Mami at the table. "All I did was eat snacks with Kiki. Peanut-butter-and-banana sandwiches. Then she wanted to bake cookies. Then we had hot chocolate with extra whipped cream. My stomach hurts. I don't know how she eats like that."

"*You* used to eat like that."

"Used to. Not anymore. How was your date?"

"I had a nice time. The restaurant was fancy. Really fancy."

"How was the food?"

Mami raised her eyebrows. "Fantastic. I had *ropa vieja* and *frijoles negros*. And they served their *patacones* with garlic: it was strong, but good. Afterward, we went for a ride in a horse-drawn carriage."

I put one hand on my hip and gave Mami my "duh" look. "Doesn't he know we have cars now?"

"It's a special thing at Central Park, silly. The horses take carriages around the park. It's very romantic."

"Whatever. Did you kiss him?"

Mami blushed and sipped her coffee.

"That's a yes?"

"Okay, this particular mother-daughter chat is over," Mami said, shooing me toward my room. "Good night, Marisol-Mariposa. *Sueños dulces*."

"I hope you have sweet dreams, too," I told her.

"Don't worry," Mami said, as she kissed me on the forehead. "I will."

7

It was Sunday afternoon and I was taking Mrs. Trader's dog, Tyson, on his daily walk. Impulsively, I turned down East 17th Street to check out all the houses with their Christmas decorations. It was still early, only the first week of December, but folks were already showing off their holiday spirit. Tyson tugged at his leash, trying to make me break into a jog. Usually I indulged him in a quick race, but I wasn't in the mood today.

"*Tranquilo*," I whispered, as he tried to take off down the block. He turned and gave me an exasperated look that said, "Don't you know this game?"

"No running today," I said firmly. Tyson barked loudly, clearly disappointed.

I bent to nuzzle his ear. "Next time. It's a promise," I told him. And I thought he understood, because he started wagging his tail cheerfully. At first, I had been a little afraid of Tyson. But soon I began to look forward to the walk almost as much as I looked forward to the crisp ten-dollar bill that Mrs. Trader gave me when I brought Tyson home.

I took my time walking down the streets, gazing at the decorations: the multicolored lights, the wreaths festooned with gold ribbons, the plastic reindeer, and Santa perched precariously on the roof of Mrs. Fisher's house. Sometimes I wondered what it would be like to live in a house like one of these, a place with an upstairs and a downstairs—and a basement! What would Mami and I do with so much space? *Fíjese.* I couldn't even imagine it.

Not that I'm complaining about where we live now. It's great. The previous summer, when Mami had gotten a promotion at work, we'd moved into the top floor of a house—a real switch from the apartment building on Ocean Avenue that I had grown up in. In our old building, things just seemed to go from bad to worse. There used to be a doorman on Ocean Avenue. I remember him from when I was little. His name was Eli and he had a big round face with a gut to match. Mami said Eli couldn't protect cheese from mice, but I liked having him there. It made me feel safe. Then one day he was gone. Just like that. The owner of the building fired him and Mami couldn't find enough tenants to chip in to hire a doorman.

Over time, the paint in the hallway faded from a bright,

clear blue to a dirty, muddy bluish brown. And when the paint started to chip, you could see that the lobby and the halls had once been green, a minty green that reminded me of hospitals and other places I didn't like to visit. When Magda and the Rosarios lived in the building, back when we were in the second grade, we had *so* much fun. Magda and I would Rollerblade around the lobby, pretending we were Olympic ice-skaters and making up spy games. Magda was really good at spy games. We'd seen this thing on TV about a cold war and since we had no idea what that meant, Magda made up a game.

"It's a cold war," she would order, in her deepest "general" voice. "Retreat to your foxhole and gather your weapons."

We'd run back to our apartments and fill our backpacks with weapons worthy of being used in a cold war. Ziploc bags full of ice cubes that we'd hurl like hand grenades at each other were a favorite. Once, Magda filled her brother's water-gun with frozen Gatorade and pummeled me. When she was done, I was covered with liquid blue gunk. I felt like a human Slurpee! But it was so much fun; I didn't even care that Mami yelled at me for getting a stain on my new sweater.

Tyson tugged at his leash—we were nearing his favorite spot. I had come to love walking him, and except for the times when he tried to pick a fight with other dogs, it was a good job. I had saved every dime Mrs. Trader had given me and had almost enough money for the *quince* dress that I wanted. I'd changed my mind about the dress. Even if I ended up having a party in Tía Alicia's basement, I wanted to wear it. It was the *quinceañera* ballgown of my dreams.

I had just dropped Tyson off and was headed home when I saw Magda walking down the street with a guy named Sammy Baldonado, from our school. They were holding hands. When Magda saw me, she broke into a grin so bright it could have lit up any Christmas tree.

"Yo, Marisol," she tossed off casually, rolling her eyes toward Sammy's barrel chest. I knew that look, that was her, "check it out, ain't it cool?" expression.

"Hey, Magda," I said. Then more shyly, I murmured, "Hi, Sammy." Sammy was the star of our high-school basketball team, a junior who was being scouted by UNC, Michael Jordan's alma mater.

"Yo," Sammy said.

"What have you guys been up to?" I asked.

"Studying," Sammy said.

"Sorta," Magda giggled. "Did you just come from my house?"

"No, I just dropped Tyson off," I said.

"Who's Tyson?" Sammy asked, interested.

Magda and I burst out laughing simultaneously.

"Tyson's the dog next door," Magda explained. "Marisol walks him every night."

"What kind of dog is he?" Sammy asked.

"A shepherd," I said, surprised. Why was Sammy being so chatty? Why didn't he just scowl and mumble "Uh-huh" like the other jocks at school?

"I've got a Rottweiler myself," Sammy said, puffing out his chest a bit.

"Ooooh," I said. But what I really was thinking was, How did Magda land a date with Sammy Baldonado?

"Well, I better be getting home," I said, shivering a little bit from the cold.

"Come over for dinner, Marisol," Magda said, releasing Sammy's hand.

Then she turned to Sammy, placing a perfectly groomed hand on his chest. "Call me tomorrow, okay?"

"You know I will," he said, cheerfully. "Bye, baby." Then he kissed her on the mouth, turned, and started to walk away.

"Nice to meet you, Marisol," he called out over his shoulder. I waved back. It was funny. Sammy Baldonado's legs were so long, it seemed that in four quick strides, he was around the corner and out of sight.

Magda grabbed my hand as we made the way up the steps to her house. "I could scream," she whispered in a scratchy voice that reminded me of Lauren Bacall in the old movies we watched.

"But you won't," I said.

"I won't," she repeated. "You know why?"

"Oh, I know why," I said, knowing what was coming, some diva line Magda had copped from an old movie.

"I'm just too, too cool, to get all hot and bothered."

"Whatever," I said, laughing.

Magda threw open the front door of her house and called out, "I'm home!" for all to hear.

"Who cares, brat?" sniped Marisol's big sister, Evelyn, as she came down the stairs.

Evelyn grabbed a fashion magazine off the pile of mail in the entryway and smiled at me. "Hey, Marisol, *qué paso?*" she said. Ever since I'd come back from Panama fluent in Spanish, all the people in our families who used to be snotty weren't so snotty anymore. It made Magda furious.

"*Y de yo?*" she asked her sister.

"*De bobo no tengo nada a ver,*" Evelyn said, as she settled into the living room sofa and flicked on her favorite *telenovela* on the Spanish language TV.

I followed Marisol into the kitchen. It didn't take two seconds of smelling the delicious spices to know that Tía Luisa was making *pernil.*

"Marisol is staying for dinner," Magda said, bussing her mother on the cheek.

"*Qué placer,*" Tía Luisa said addressing me. "We love having you and as you can see, there's plenty of food. Don't forget to call your mom."

I reached for the kitchen phone and dialed the number to my house.

"Hello?" a male voice answered.

"Sorry, wrong number," I said and hung up the phone.

I dialed the number again and this time got Mami.

"*Hola, como estás?*" I said. "I'm going to stay at Magda's for dinner."

"That's fine," Mami answered. "Did you just call and hang up?"

"Yeah," I said, confused. "Some weird guy answered the phone."

"That was Eduardo," she answered.

"So you go out *once* and he's answering the phone?" I said, my voice dripping with disgust. I knew from the look that Tía Luisa gave me that I was being *fresca* and she was eavesdropping.

"Watch yourself," Mami said, the warning in her voice clear. "He was calling in to the hospital and he heard the other line click so he answered it. But I don't owe you an explanation, young lady."

"Okay, okay," I said, backing off. Besides, I'd made my point. "I'll come home right after dinner."

"Will Luisa drive you?" Mami asked.

"Mami, Tía Luisa is too busy to chauffeur me around," I said, annoyed. "I'll just walk home."

"I will drive you," Tía Luisa called out, as she added more seasoning to the ham sizzling on the stove.

"She said she'll drive me," I said, into the receiver.

"Make sure you say 'thank you,'" Mami intoned.

"I always do," I said, getting testy again. "Okay? Bye."

"Magda's gone up to her room," Tía Luisa said, *"Pero dame un momentito, quiero hablar contigo."*

Tía Luisa poured coconut water into the pot of rice and peas, but she kept her gaze on me. I knew that look. Mami and Tía Luisa had been friends since Panama; she was practically like a second mom to me. I knew from her look that she was in *la moda de Mami* and she was going to give me a lecture.

"You know it's been a long time since your mom has been out with a nice guy," she said. *"Debes ser más tranquila sobre eso."*

I didn't need Tía Luisa to tell me to cut Mami some slack. *"Yo sé,"* I said. "I know."

"Does it bother you that your Mami is dating again?" Tía Luisa asked, handing me a cup of juice.

"No—it does—not." Though I tried to make my voice sound more even, each word came out like a punch.

"Your Mami is still a young woman," Tía Luisa said. "She should date."

"I know," I muttered, looking at the floor.

"Okay, *dame un beso,*" Tía Luisa said, pointing to her cheek.

I gave her a quick kiss. "I'm going to find Magda."

"You girls don't be long," Tía Luisa said as she returned to stirring the pot on the stove. "Dinner won't be long."

I bounded up the stairs two at a time and knocked on the door to Magda's room. Not surprisingly, she was sitting at Evelyn's vanity table, applying makeup.

"What's up?" I said, plopping on the bed. "How did you hook up with Sammy Baldonado? He's so cute. Nice, too. I like that."

"I know," Magda said, hugging herself. "I can't believe my luck."

I didn't want to sound stupid, but there was something I really wanted to know.

"Magda, do you ever think some guys are out of your league?"

"What kind of a question is that?"

"I mean—you went out with Sammy Baldonado, one of the coolest guys in school. But I wouldn't think he was out of your league, because you're one of the coolest freshman in school."

"Thanks," Magda said, full of pride. "That's *so* nice of you to say."

"But if I wanted to go out with a guy like Sammy, then you'd think, Fat chance, right?"

"You like Sammy?" Magda said, spinning around to face me.

"No," I said, exasperated. Sometimes Magda could be so self-involved. "I just mean if I ever liked a guy as cool as that, then I'd never have a chance, right? It's just the universal law. Jocks go out with cool girls. And nerdy girls date nerdy guys, you know what I mean?"

"What about the boyfriend you had in Panama?" Magda asked. "He was nowhere near a nerd." I smiled, thinking about Rubén. "He was a total honey, I remember."

"But sometimes I think going to Panama was totally different," I said. "It was like a dream where I got to play this role."

"Then play the role here," Magda said. "That's all it takes."

I mulled the idea over in my head for a few minutes and wondered which guy I would go for, if I could go out with any guy at school.

"So where'd you meet Sammy, anyway?" I asked, kicking off my sneakers and swinging my legs onto Magda's bed.

"I met him at a party last night," Magda said.

"What party?" I asked, picking up a copy of *Seventeen* magazine and trying to sound nonchalant.

"My bad," Magda said, putting her hand over her mouth. "It was just this party that me and Marisa and Elizabeth went to."

"Nice of you to invite me," I said, tossing the magazine onto the floor.

"You were baby-sitting. Besides, I didn't really know the guys who threw the party," Magda said, apologetically. "They were friends of Marisa's."

"I get it," I said. "So Marisa is your best friend now? I can't stand that *boricua* cow."

"Don't start, Marisol," Magda said, rolling her eyes. "You're the one who went away for a whole year. I made other friends. I can't just drop them now that you're back."

"I was—" I started to say that she has always known that I would come back. But then I thought of Ana, the girl who had become my closest friend in Panama. If our situation had been reversed, and Magda had moved down to Panama, no way would I have ditched Ana.

"So my *mami*'s new boyfriend is just buck wild," I huffed, changing the subject. "When I called, he answered the phone, *fíjese*."

"He's got a lot of nerve! Who does he think he is?" Magda said, taking my side so quickly that I knew she was trying to make up with me.

"Your mom said that I should chill out," I went on. "It's been a long time since my *mami* has had a boyfriend."

"So? That doesn't mean he should be pushing himself all up in the spot. Answering the phone and what not," she said, waving her hand in the air. "*Irascible.* Next thing you know, he'll have a set of keys and he'll be getting his mail at your house."

"*No me digas!*" I groaned. "Let's not go there. Can you imagine having to share a bathroom with some weird guy?"

"You forget that I have three brothers?" Magda said, laughing. "But share my bathroom with a total stranger? No way, José."

"Evelyn, Magdalena, Marisol, Rogelio, Danilo," Tía Luisa called from the bottom of the stairs. "Who eats, eats now."

"Don't worry about your Mami's *novio.* It'll all work out," Magda said. "And I'm sorry I didn't invite you to the party."

"Whatever," I said, shrugging my shoulders and looking away. I thought about the way Marisa had dissed me the other day. Was she making fun of me at the party, too?

"Marisol! Magdalena!" Tío Ricardo bellowed up the stairs. "*Nosotros te esperamos.*"

"Hungry?" Magda asked, putting her arm around my shoulder and giving it a squeeze.

I thought about saying no, but I couldn't very well sit sulking in Magda's room.

"Come on, Marisol," Magda said. "If we don't come down, my *papi*'s going to have a heart attack. You know how he gets."

She took my hand and started to skip down the steps just the way we had when we were little girls. I couldn't help but follow her. By the bottom of the stairwell, we were giggling uncontrollably over nothing at all. Funny, isn't it? How you can grow closer and grow apart from someone at the very same time?

8

The following Sunday morning, Mami and I attended Spanish service at Our Lady of Refuge, the Catholic church down the street from our house. Ever since I had come back from Panama, there had been little ways in which Mami treated me differently. Before I went, when I spoke more Spanglish than Spanish, we always went to the English service at church. Now we went to the Spanish service. To tell the truth, a lot of it still went over my head, but I liked Padre Delano, the Spanish priest. He was younger than the American priests, with a shaved bald head that made him look more like a basketball player than a priest. And the little *chismes* he told during his sermon made the whole congregation laugh.

As we entered the church, I dipped my fingers in the holy water, crossed myself, and followed Mami into the pew. We were early, as usual. Mami knelt upon the red velvet altar and silently began to pray. I knelt beside her and tried to think about what to say. "Marisol-Mariposa, don't just ask God for stuff. We're Catholics, not stuff-ologists," Mami had told me when I was little and prayed every night for a brand-new Barbie doll and for a Barbie dream house to go with it. "What you tell God is between you and God, but *querida*, a prayer is more than a holy shopping list," she had said, holding me in her arms. "Always give thanks for the food on your plate and the roof over your head. Pray not just for yourself, but for the ones you love. *Recuerdas, hija*, it's not about an open hand, but an open heart."

As I prayed, I thought about my friendship with Magda. How could she be my *mejor amiga* and go to parties without me? How could she roll with a girl like Marisa and tell her things about me behind my back? I reached up to touch the little gold cross that I wore everyday, the one that was the exact replica of the one Magda wore. I hadn't changed since we were little girls, but Magda had. What I kept wondering was, could I change to keep up with her? Could we both change and still be *mejores amigas*?

Watching Mami pray, her fingers nimbly following the rosary in her hand, I tried not to be a stuff-ologist. But the truth was that I also had stuff on my mind—the dress I'd seen at the mall, a *quinceañera* ballroom and a buffet full of food, invitations with gold lettering announcing my fifteenth birthday, and my giant step into womanhood. "God," I mouthed silently, as I closed my eyes and bent my head to the wooden pew in front of me. "I want to have a *quince*, but I don't know how it will happen. If it's the right thing, please make my dream come true."

Then I continued. "Thank you, God, for Mami. For Tía China and all the *tías*. For my *abuela*. For Magda. Keep them safe. Amen."

I sat up, but Mami was still praying. I watched the outline of her head, the soft flutter of her eyelashes as she blinked beneath closed lids. I knew that Mami prayed for me. In or out of church, she said *benediciones* for me, a gazillion times a day. Is that how mothers love? Not only by telling their kids that they love them, but by taking every wish they have for you straight to the ears of God?

After church, we walked out to find everything covered in white. It was almost as if we were living in one of those plastic souvenir things and God had shaken it, making the snow come down.

"Excellent," I said, letting the flakes fall, one by one, onto by gloved hand.

At the gate, I turned toward our house, but Mami stopped me.

She pointed across the street at a tan Pathfinder truck that I recognized.

"Eduardo is waiting," she said.

"Thanks for the advance notice," I muttered.

"One, I wasn't sure if he was going to get off early from the hospital," Mami said. "Two, I don't owe you an explanation."

Eduardo spotted us, beeped his horn, then waved. Mami and I crossed the street toward him.

"*Hola, cariño,*" Mami said, kissing Eduardo on the mouth. It wasn't a quick kiss, either.

"Hey, Eduardo, what's up?" I said, opening the back door to the car and hopping in.

"*Buenos días, Marisolita,*" Eduardo said, turning on the car ignition as Mami and I buckled up.

Every hair on my back stood up. He kept calling me Marisolita; he said it was a sign of affection. As if.

"You know no one calls me Marisolita," I said, sticking my head toward the front of the car.

"You know I'm just joshing ya', Mar y Sol," Eduardo said, laughing. I hated his laugh. It was a goofy *heh-heh-heh* that came dangerously close to sounding fake, if you ask me.

"I think it's cute, Marisol-Mariposa," Mami said.

"Can we just quit it with the nicknames, for now?" I asked. "Are you guys going out?"

"We are going out and Tía China is coming over to braid your hair," Mami explained.

"She is?" I screamed. I'd been asking Tía China to braid my hair for weeks, but she was always so busy at the hair salon where she worked. She said the last thing she wanted to do on her day off was touch a single hair on anybody's head.

"I talked to her last night. She didn't say anything about coming over."

"It was supposed to be a surprise, but since you're so nosy . . ." Mami said. "She'll be at the house by two o'clock."

"I figured I'd take your mother to a movie," Eduardo said. "That is, if it's okay with you."

Then he laughed his goofy laugh again.

"Heh, heh, heh," I said, mocking him. Then I silently made an L with my forefinger and my thumb. What a loser.

The minute we got home, Eduardo walked over to the television and turned it to ESPN, the sports station. Who did he think he was, just walking around our apartment like he owned it? I stood there, giving him the evil eye, but he didn't notice it. Unfortunately, Mami did.

"Marisol," she said, pulling me into the kitchen. "I've had a hard week, and I'm not in the mood to get into it with you. I'm trying to be sensitive to how you feel about Eduardo. But think about me. Don't I deserve to have some fun?"

"Of course you do," I said. "But he's so goofy."

At first she looked vexed, then she got a playful look in her eye.

"Well, we can't all date guys *tan suave como su novio*, Rubén."

"He was pretty cute," I said, smiling at the memory of my Panamanian boyfriend. He had caramel-colored skin and dreadlocks, like a reggae singer. He was tall, taller than me. And let me tell you, few guys are. We danced together *el baile típico* in a Christmas concert. I wore a traditional costume and Mami and Magda came down from New York to see me.

Sometimes when I closed my eyes at night, I could feel how it felt to kiss him. But the longer I was away, the harder it was to remember how it felt exactly. Sometimes, I closed my eyes and I couldn't feel a thing. I could just see his face above mine, circling like a plane about to land.

"I miss him," I said, softly.

"I know," Mami said, cradling my head to her chest. "Now imagine how lonely you would feel if you didn't have another *novio* for years and years."

"That's how you feel?" I asked, looking into Mami's sweet, smiling face.

She nodded. "So give me a break about Eduardo, okay?"

"Okay," I said, hugging her back. "But I'm keeping an eye on you."

"Don't I know it," she said. "Now I'm going to watch TV with Eduardo." She took two beers out of the fridge and went into the living room.

It was just after three o'clock when Tía China rang the door-bell.

"Okay, *hija*. Be good," Mami said, kissing me on the cheek. "Don't let China experiment too much with your hair. You've got to be presentable for school."

"I've got it," I said, holding the door open for Mami and Eduardo to leave.

"See you later, Marisoli—" Eduardo said.

I scowled at hearing the *ita* that he was about to add to my name.

"Fooled ya," he said, giving my shoulder a squeeze. "Heh, heh, heh."

"Heh, heh, heh," I repeated through clenched teeth.

Seconds later, Tía China bounded through the front door. She's Mami's youngest sister and my favorite aunt. Her name is spelled China, like the country, but it's pronounced "Cheena," the Spanish way.

"*Hola, mi amor,*" Tía China said, leaving a big red lipstick mark on my cheek.

"I'm so glad you came!" I said, locking the door behind her.

Tía China always had a different hairstyle. At the moment, her hair was short like a boy's and blond. Of course, it looked fabulous on her.

She plopped two plastic bags of synthetic hair on the table and nodded toward them.

"Listen, *niña,*" she said, wryly. "If anyone asks if that's really your hair, you tell 'em, 'It's mine. I bought it!'"

I laughed and opened the bags. The hair was a beautiful reddish brown.

"Did Mami say I could have this color?!" I asked.

"What color? I thought that was your hair color!" Tía China said, feigning innocence. "Come on, let's get your hair done before she gets home."

I turned on the stereo to a hip-hop station and sat cross-legged on the living room floor in front of Tía China.

"I love this song!" she said, snapping her fingers to the beat.

"Me, too," I said, moving my shoulders up and down.

Tía China took a comb and began to unravel the twists in my hair.

"*Boricua, morena*," Tía China sang, following along the chorus. A *Boricua* is a Puerto Rican. A *morena* is a dark-skinned girl. It was kind of me and Tía China's anthem. She was wearing a navy blue velvet shirt, with three buttons undone. As she swayed to the music, her arm full of silver bracelets tinkled.

I made my voice deeper and rapped the guy's part, "I'm not a *playa*, but I crush a lot!"

Both Tía China and I laughed.

"Speaking of players," Tía China said. "Inez's new *novio* is kinda cute."

"Ugh," I groaned.

"Come on," she said, tugging on my hair with the comb. "Be nice."

I made a face. "He's such a cheeseball."

"Do you see the way he looks at your mother?" Tía China asked. "He *adores* her."

"He called me Marisolita," I sniped.

Tía China laughed, "That's so cute! Maybe I'll call you Marisolita, too—"

I jabbed her with my elbow. "Don't even think about it!"

"Eduardo's silly sense of humor is not what's really bothering you," Tía China said.

I tried to think of a good reason why Mami shouldn't be with Eduardo, but I couldn't. Instead, I sat in silence while Tía China combed out my hair.

"*Venga a la cocina,*" Tía China said, standing up. "Let me wash this bush."

I paused to look at myself in the hallway mirror; all combed out, my hair was like a big, fuzzy Afro.

"I think this is a really hip style," I said, vamping in front of the mirror.

"I *love* it!" Tía China said, throwing her arms around my neck. "It's so retro-chic."

Tía China washed my hair and we went back into the living room.

"It's gonna take forever, isn't it?" I asked, pulling a cushion off the sofa and sitting down on top of it.

"*Las cosas se hacen bien hechas . . .*" Tía China carped.

"*O no se hacen,*" I recited, finishing Abuela's favorite expression.

"I want the braids to be thick like the girls in the music videos," I said.

"I know the style," Tía China said.

"And I want them down to here," I said, pointing to my elbow.

"That's a little long, *niña!*"

"But that's the style!" I insisted.

"Okay, master, your wish is my command," Tía China said, crossing both arms and bowing her head like "I Dream of Jeannie."

"Very funny."

After Tía China had done the first braid and I pulled it in front of me. "Perfect," I said, approvingly. I couldn't wait till Magda saw it.

"*Por supuesto, lo hice yo!*" Tía China said. "Only the best for my favorite niece."

"Am I really your favorite?" I asked.

"You know you are," Tía China said, squeezing me on the shoulder. "Just don't tell Roxana."

"I won't," I said, grinning. "Do you really think I'm being a brat about this Eduardo thing?"

"You are being a total and complete brat," Tía China said. "But I understand."

"I looked for my father, you know," I explained. "When I was in Panama, I went to where he used to live."

"If your mother knew, she'd *kill* you," Tía China said.

"I left a letter with his brother," I said. "But he never showed up. He never came to see me."

"He probably never even saw it, *cariña.*"

"The worse thing is not knowing. Not knowing where he is, if he loves me, if he thinks about me," I said, looking out the window. Then I felt myself shiver as if it were snowing inside, instead of outside.

"I wish I could tell you that he did love you, that he misses you," Tía China said, quietly. "But you're a young woman now. I can tell you, honestly, that all you can do is love someone. You can't force them to stay. You can't force them to love you back."

"He's like this big question mark in my life," I said. "I can't think about having a new father when I don't even know where my real father is."

"*Mucho apura traye cansancio,*" Tía China said. "Don't rush things! The question isn't whether or not Eduardo will make a good dad for you. Right now, your mom is just trying to decide if he would make a good boyfriend."

"I guess that's not such a big deal," I said, fingering the thick braids that fell like ropes onto my shoulders. "Thanks for listening to me gripe, Tía China."

"*De nada, niña,*" Tía China said. "So what's the latest on your *quince*? I hear you don't want to have it in Tía Alicia's basement."

"Was she offended?" I asked, looking up. "I didn't mean to be rude about it."

"It's okay," Tía China said. "But you need to come up with another plan."

"I know," I said. "Right now, I'm just praying for a miracle."

"I believe in miracles," Tía China said, making the sign of a cross, then kissing her crossed fingers. She shook her wrists and stood up from the sofa. "Ooo, all that braiding is making my hands hurt. Why don't we take a break and order a pizza?"

Tía China and I had finished off a pizza, finished my hair, and were halfway through watching *Titanic* on video when Mami came home.

"*Hola!*" Mami called out as she entered the living room. "I'm home."

"Have a good time?" Tía China said.

"Couldn't have been better," Mami said, beaming.

I started to roll my eyes, but Tía China stepped on my foot.

"What did you do?" I asked, in the sweetest voice I could muster.

"You're going to think it's silly," Mami said, sinking into her favorite overstuffed chair.

"A date with Eduardo? Silly?"

"We went ice-skating at Rockefeller Center," Mami said. "Then we went to a movie. Then we had hamburgers at the All-Star Sports Café. Eduardo *loves* the All-Star Sports Café."

"Wow, *muy divertido*," Tía China said.

"Yeah," I admitted. "Sounds like fun."

"I like your hair," Mami said, fingering the thick braids. "The color is a little lighter than I expected."

I pointed to Tía China. "It wasn't me!"

"No, the color is pretty. It brightens your face."

"Thank you," I said, spinning around so Mami could see my braids from all sides.

"I almost forgot!" Mami said, jumping up out of her chair. "Eduardo sent a present for you."

She handed me a bag and I looked over at Tía China.

"What is it?" I asked, nervously. What if it was one of Eduardo's silly gags, like a lump of plastic vomit?

"It's a basketball," I said, opening the bag. "It's a WNBA original, signed by all the players. This is *really* cool."

"All net!" Tía China said, faking a slam dunk.

"Eduardo's just trying to get on my good side," I told Mami. I held the ball at arm's length and examined it suspiciously.

"You bet," she said, brightly.

"Well, tell him I said thanks, okay?"

"You can tell him yourself. He's coming to dinner next Friday." Mami said. "That is, if it's okay with you?"

I tried to spin the basketball on one finger but had no luck. It dropped and I picked it up, admiring the signatures of all my favorite players.

"It's fine with me," I said.

Across the room, Tía China gave me a wink and a smile.

9

Saturday afternoon, Mami and I rode the subway into the city to see an exhibit of Diego Rivera murals at MOMA, the Museum of Modern Art. Going to the museum was always Mami's special treat for me. Ever since I was a little girl, if I got a good report card and Mami had the money, we would ride the subway into the city and go to a museum. There were so many in New York and we'd been to almost all of them: the Guggenheim; the Cloisters; the Metropolitan Museum, which Mami called "The Met"; the New Museum and the Natural History Museum. Closer to home, there was the Brooklyn Museum, with its funky Egyptian collection, which I loved. There was a Children's Museum, too, but I had never liked it, even when I was a little kid.

Entering MOMA, I always felt a little intimidated. It was such a big, fancy place, with some of the greatest works of arts that have ever been created. There were guards everywhere, and they made me nervous. Ever since I was a little girl, I knew not to touch the paintings, but I liked to get really close—to see how the paint stuck to the canvas, to try to guess how many times the painter had painted over that same blue or yellow spot. The minute I put my face right up against the painting, there would be some mean old guard reminding me, "Young lady, don't touch the paintings." I would *never* touch a painting. But there was a part of me that secretly believed that if I could get close enough to a painting, maybe I could walk right into it, like Alice through the looking glass.

Mami bought the tickets and handed one to me.

"*Vámonos*. It's on the second floor."

"I'm so excited."

"Me, too."

"Diego Rivera was a Mexican painter, famous for his huge murals," Mami explained as we entered the first gallery. "*Venga*, there's something I want to show you."

Mami walked up to a gigantic painting. It was called *Distributing Arms*.

"It's about war," I said, as I looked at all the men and women in military dress. "I don't like it."

"Yes, it is," Mami said. "But at the time, Diego Rivera was very interested in Communism. Do you see that girl?"

Mami pointed to a beautiful girl wearing a red shirt and a star.

"That's Frida Kahlo. She was Diego Rivera's wife, and a brilliant painter herself."

"Wife?" I asked. "She doesn't look much older than me."

"Hmm," Mami said. "She wasn't. She was probably about nineteen when she posed for this painting."

"She only has one eyebrow," I laughed. "One big bushy eyebrow across her face. Did she really look like that? Or was that a painter thing?"

Mami laughed. "No, she really looked like that. Still, *era bellísima, no?*"

I nodded in agreement. "She really is beautiful."

We walked through the exhibit, stopping to read the cards under each one. Several of the paintings featured Frida Kahlo. I liked the Diego Rivera murals, but I wanted to know more about Frida, the painter girl with the striking face.

"These paintings make me think of Panama," I told Mami, as we left the final room of the exhibition.

"That makes sense," Mami said. "Mexico, like Panama, is a Central American country. There are specific things that are different, but we share many things in common."

"Can I get a couple of Diego Rivera postcards at the bookstore?"

"*Claro.* We'll get one to send to your *abuela,* too."

At the museum bookstore, there were a gazillion postcards of different paintings. At home, I had a blank book where I glued the postcards in, and in purple marker underneath, I would write the name of the painting, the artist, and the date when it was painted. I call it my art collection.

"That was fun, Mami," I said as we walked out onto 53rd Street. Mami turned left toward the Serendipity Sweet Shop and I followed her. You could get the most chocolatey hot chocolate there. I could just about taste it. But first, I stopped to give Mami a kiss on the cheek.

"*Gracias*, Mami."

"You're welcome, Marisol-Mariposa. You know you've always loved museums. When you were a baby, I used to wheel you around the Guggenheim. Even if you were crying, by the time we got to the top floor, you were as quiet as a mouse."

The Guggenheim is another one of my and Mami's favorite museums. It's a round building, and when you stand in the lobby, you can look up and see that each floor is a circle, like the rings of Saturn. It was funny trying to picture Mami wheeling a baby carriage round and round the museum floors.

"You never told me that story," I said.

"There are lots of things I've never told you."

"Was my *papi* there?"

"Where?"

"At the museum, Mami. When I was a baby," I said. Mami always started to tune out when I asked questions about my father.

"He was still in our lives, if that's what you mean. But he wasn't with us at the museum. He always said it was a waste of time and money."

A waste of time? A waste of money? I bit my lip and looked down at all the fancy shops along Fifth Avenue. Since

I loved to draw and loved to look at paintings, I had always imagined that Papi was an art lover, too. It was kind of shocking to find out that he wasn't. This was exactly the sort of thing that scared me about finding him. Because I knew so little about him, I just made things up. But I had been filling in the blanks for so long that I couldn't tell what was truth and what was fantasy. And when I find out that the truth is harder, not as sweet, sometimes I think, I don't really want to know.

"So if my *papi* didn't like art, what did he like?"

"Oh, Marisol," Mami groaned. "Must we do this?"

I thought about how much fun we'd had at the museum and how much I was looking forward to the hot chocolate at Serendipity. This was shaping up to be just about a perfect day. I didn't want to ruin it by getting Mami into a bad mood.

"I'm sorry, it's no big deal," I said, softly.

Mami put both of her gloved hands on my cheeks. My face felt cold and warm at the same time. Warm where Mami's hands covered me, cold everywhere else.

"I know you want to find your *papi*. I know that you want to know everything about him. It's just that . . ."

Her voice trailed off and she looked away.

"It's just that . . ."

I looked into her eyes and I saw they were wet with tears. I had ruined it. We were having a perfect day and now Mami was crying.

"It's okay, Mami," I said, wiping a tear from her cheek. *"Vamos por los dulces."*

Then I told her what she had always told me when I was a little girl and got into a sad mood: "Nothing wrong with you that chocolate can't fix."

"Exactly," Mami said, forcing a smile and taking my hand.

We walked past a construction site and watched for a second while planks of steel were welded together. A cool guy in a jeep drove by blasting hip-hop music. I heard the strains of Tía China's favorite: *"Boricua, morena."* Tourists prattled in Japanese, German, and Italian, snapping pictures and gawking at the Midtown skyscrapers. All around us, city sounds boomed. But Mami and I walked the rest of the way in silence.

Sitting underneath the Art Déco lamps at Serendipity, Mami and I toasted each other with our glass hot chocolate mugs. Then we played our favorite Serendipity game, where we each tried to come up with the most toasts.

"To the best *hija* in the world," Mami said as our mugs clinked.

"To the best *mami* in the world," I responded.

"To hot chocolate."

"To cold chocolate."

"Hmmm. Cold chocolate. Chocolate milk or chocolate ice-cream?" Mami said, giggling.

"To chocolate ice-cream." I said, taking another sip.

"To Diego Rivera."

"To Frida Kahlo."

"To women painters."

"To bushy eyebrows."

"To Mexico."

"To Panama."

"To *la patria*."

"To art."

"To *quinces*," Mami said, kissing me on the cheek. "Some way, somehow."

"To *quinces*," I agreed.

Later, when Mami got up to go to the bathroom, I made one last toast. "To Papi. Some way, somehow." I whispered as I raised my mug in the air. Then I emptied the last of the sweet, hot chocolate into my mouth.

10

I didn't want to go to Lily Nunez's *quinceañera*. For one, I hardly knew her. She went to Catholic school instead of to the public school with me and Magda. We didn't really like her. It wasn't that she wasn't nice, it was just that she was the kind of girl that our *mami*s always compared us to. "Did you know that Lily is attending a computer camp at MIT?" Mami would ask. "Did you hear that Lily won first prize in the science fair?" Lily's mother had gone to school with Mami and Tía Luisa in Panama, so we saw them at our summer picnics and all the holiday gatherings.

The day of Lily's *quince*, I tried to pretend that I was sick. It was Saturday afternoon and I stayed in bed all morning until Mami came looking for me.

She knocked on the door. *"Qué pasa?"* Mami asked. "You've been so quiet this morning."

"I don't feel well," I groaned.

Mami came over and sat on the bed. "What's wrong?"

"I've got really bad cramps."

Mami raised one eyebrow, then another. "Again?"

"What do you mean, again?" I asked, offended.

"You just had your period last week, Marisol-Mariposa," she said. "You don't want to go to Lily's *quince* tonight."

I shook my head no.

"Come on, get up, *preciosa*," Mami said, pulling the covers off me. "Let's talk about this over lunch."

I padded into the dining room in my pajamas and slippers. A few minutes later, Mami came out with a plate of tuna sandwiches, with relish, just the way I liked them.

"Why don't you want to go to Lily's *quince?*" Mami asked, as she bit into her sandwich.

"Because . . ."

"That's not an answer, Marisol," she said, sternly.

"I barely know her," I insisted.

Mami put down her sandwich and scrunched her mouth to one side. "You've known Lily since you were a baby."

"But I only know her because you're friends with her mother."

"And?"

"Aaa-nnn-ddd," I said, huffily, drawing out the word as long as possible. "That doesn't make me friends with her."

Mami covered her eyes with her hands for a second, then she said, "It may not make you friends, Marisol. But the fact that we've known Lily and her family all these years, the fact that we're all from Panama, does make us a *community*. It means that we show up at each other's christenings, birthdays, and funerals. Remember that word, Marisol. Community. It may not mean much to you now, but it will mean something to you later. I promise."

I ate the second half of my sandwich in silence. "May I be excused?" I asked.

Mami shook her head no. "I think there's another reason you don't want to go tonight."

I looked at her quizzically. "Okay. Since you can read my mind, what is it?"

Mami's voice softened then and she said, "You don't want to go to Lily's *quince*, because right now, it looks like I won't be able to afford to give you your own."

I didn't want to admit it, but Mami had read my mind. The thought of watching Lily at her *quince*, when I wasn't even sure I could have one, made me sick. I was so jealous of her! I couldn't say it, but I could feel it like a stone at the bottom of my stomach.

Mami reached out and cupped my face with both of her hands. "It's okay to feel envious," she said. "It's not okay to stay home and feel sorry for yourself. Do you understand?"

I nodded my head yes and went back into my room. I crawled under the covers of my bed and flipped through the pages of my *quinceañera* dream book. Maybe I should go ahead and have my *quince* in Tía Alicia's basement. Maybe a budget *quince* was better than no *quince* at all.

That night, Mami and I rode with Tía Luisa and Magda over to the Community Center up in Orchard Beach, in the Bronx. There must have been over one hundred people there. We found the table with our names and I fingered the pretty place cards. There was a picture of an Easter lily on mine and my name was written in a beautiful golden script. This is where I sit, I thought. Then looking around at the room full of Panamanians, I thought, And this is where I belong. I began to understand what Mami meant when she talked about community.

"I'm starvin' like Marvin," Magda said, giving my arm a tug. She looked amazing in a white sleeveless dress that she'd inherited from her big sister. I was wearing a pink dress with puffy sleeves that had looked cute in the hallway mirror at home, but somehow seemed dorky here at the Community Center.

I followed Magda to the buffet table. We both nodded approvingly at the spread that was laid before us. There was *arroz con pollo*, rice and peas, black beans, and *plátanos*. The potato salad was made Panamanian style with olives and mustard. When Magda and I saw that there was a whole other table piled sky-high with desserts, we grabbed two plates: one for regular food, one for dulces. We were stuffed before they even wheeled out the birthday cake.

Different people gave speeches about what a saint Lily

was and what a fine young woman she was already becoming. Her mother gave a speech about her own *quince* in Panama that left all the *mamis* in tears. Her older brother made a toast, as did countless cousins. When her high-school science teacher got up to speak, Magda and I exchanged looks and headed for the bathroom.

In the bathroom, Magda reapplied her striking red lipstick and I tried to squeeze some glamor out of the pinkish lip gloss that was the only thing that Mami would let me wear.

"We better get back," I said to Magda. "We don't want to miss the presentation of the court."

Magda rolled her eyes. "Like I care?"

"Come on," I said, tugging her arm.

A few moments after we sat down, the lights were dimmed. A giant ceramic lily was rolled into the middle of the stage. As the notes of a traditional *bachata* drifted through the air, Lily emerged from the giant lily. In traditional *quinceañera* fashion, a court of seven boys and seven girls lined up on either side of her. The girls wore buttercup yellow floor-length gowns that were just a shade paler than the sunshine satin dress Lily wore. The boys wore tuxedos. As Lily walked down the aisle between her courtiers, each boy handed her a long-stemmed calla lily. By the time she had reached the end of the row, her arms were full of them.

I was surprised at how impressed I was by the ceremony. The boys were just regular knuckleheads from the *barrio*. Since most of them were Panamanian, I'd known them since

I was a baby. But somehow, in their tuxedos, they were transformed from *barrio* boys to *caballeros*.

"The guys look good, huh?" I whispered to Magda.

She just sucked her teeth and muttered, "Whatever."

"Come on," I whispered. "José Vila is kinda cute."

She sized up his curly Afro and dark skin. "He's all right," she said. "But Reginaldo is such a mama's boy. And look at his skin."

She was right. Reginaldo had *terrible* acne.

Lily handed the bouquet of flowers to her mother, who hadn't stopped crying all night. Then a slow *baile típico* came on. It was a song I knew well, an old-fashioned love song about a woman whose lover has returned from many months at sea. The dance floor cleared and Lily danced the first dance with her father.

"Dancing with your father," Magda said, tugging my sleeve. "How dorky can you get?"

But I didn't move. I didn't say a word. In that very instant, I wanted nothing more than to be Lily in her yellow satin dress. I wanted it to be *my* legs swaying beneath the full skirt and the layers of tulle like the costume of a prima ballerina.

Lily moved in perfect rhythm with her father, as if they'd been practicing for months. She smiled at him and he smiled back. When he kissed her cheek, I wished I could feel my *papi*'s stubbly cheek against mine. All the hundreds and hundreds of times that Mami had kissed me good-night—this is what I missed, not having a *papi*. If I had known my father, if

I had been able to find him when I went to Panama, perhaps this is what I would have found: a stubbly cheek and a deep knowledge, every time he kissed me good-night, that one day I would save the first dance of my *quinceañera* just for him.

Most of the time, I did fine without a *papi*. Mami said you can't miss what you've never had. And most of the time, it was true. I knew there were men who love me like a *papi* would. I have Magda's dad, Tío Ricardo. I have my own uncles as well. But at Lily's *quinceañera*, I felt the loss of my own *papi* so deeply. There were so many things I didn't have. I didn't have the money to buy the *quince* dress I loved at the mall. Mami didn't have the money to rent a big banquet hall like this one in Orchard Beach. But worse than any of that was closing my eyes and picturing myself: dancing the first dance of the *quinceañera*, all alone.

The song seemed to go on forever. Lily buried her pretty face in her *papi*'s broad chest. I tried to keep myself from crying by remembering funny things, like the time Magda and I poured raspberry vinaigrette into her sister Evelyn's bathwater. She smelled like salad dressing for *hours*. Normally, just the word "raspberry" was enough to send me and Magda into a fit of the giggles. But that didn't work. I started crying and I stared straight ahead, hoping that no one could see me. Then I dropped my head onto the table and crossed my arms, as if I had a headache or had fallen asleep. But Mami knew.

"*No te preocupes, farolito,*" she whispered into my ear. "I know it hurts."

When the DJ started playing American music, I let Magda drag me to the dance floor. I even danced a slow dance with José Vila after big-mouth Magda told him that I liked him. I congratulated Lily, and her parents said they were looking forward to my *quinceañera*, which was sweet. But the hurt didn't go away. For days after, every time I thought about my missing *papi*, I felt this dull ache as if I'd accidentally bumped my heart against a brick wall. Then I'd think about how Mami had whispered to me at Lily's *quince*, how she just *knew* what was wrong, without my saying a single word, made me love her all the more.

11

I was sitting at the kitchen table, drinking hot chocolate with one hand and flipping through a magazine with another. Mami breezed through and gave me a kiss on the cheek.

"*Tarde. Como siempre.* Why am I always so late? I've got to work on that," she said, strapping on her watch. "Tía Alicia needs you to baby-sit Jason. It's Diego's and her wedding anniversary. Can you go to her house after you finish walking Tyson tonight?"

"No problem," I said. "I walk Tyson at six. I'll be done by six-thirty. How should I get there? Take the train?

"No, why don't I have Tía China pick you up at Mrs. Trader's?"

"Why would she come all the way over here to take me all the way back to Tía Alicia's, then go home?"

"She has her boyfriend's car. She's offering to give everybody a ride these days."

"Okay," I shrugged. "See you later."

Mami gave me a *besito*, then flew through the door. "Have a good day, *preciosa*."

I stood in front of the pharmacy waiting for Magda and trying to keep warm by pacing back and forth. I was just about to leave when she ran down the block.

"*Estoy aquí!*" she said. "I'm here! Let the party begin!"

"You're awfully cheery for seven-thirty in the morning."

"You would be too if your *mami* finally agreed to let you have the *quince* dress that you've been wanting for months."

"*No me digas.* The black dress at the mall? How'd you talk Tía Luisa into it?"

"I didn't. Papi did. He told her that she was trying to control everything about my *quince* because she never had one. He said I only turned fifteen once and that I should wear what I want."

"How did Tía Luisa take that?"

"Not well. But last night, we went to the mall and bought the dress. It's being altered today and I can pick it up after three. Will you come with me?"

"*Claro.* I can hardly wait!" I said, trying to act cheerful. But inside I felt miserable. I tried not to be jealous of Magda, but it wasn't easy.

History class was the only class that I had with Magda. Unfortunately, Marisa and Elizabeth were in the class too. I'd taken to sitting in the front, just so I didn't have to look at them. Usually, Magda sat next to me or right behind me so I could hear her little snide comments about things like the Peloponnesian war.

Mrs. Daniels was one of my favorite teachers. She was African American, with a short curly Afro that reminded me of Mami's. She was young, and always wore hip pantsuits with cool little T-shirts underneath instead of the formal shirts and dresses that the other teachers wore.

"Class, I understand that many of you girls will be having *quinceañera* or Sweet Fifteen celebrations this year."

"Some of us, not all of us," Marisa called out. I turned around and she glared at me. Ever since I'd told Magda I didn't want a double *quince*, Marisa had been getting in little jabs. But after the things Magda had said to Marisa, about my being poor and stuff, I just couldn't go for it. As things stood, I still hadn't decided what I'd do. Mami had said I could have a party in Tía Alicia's basement, or, if I wanted to save the money, we could take a trip instead.

I was thinking about going to Washington, D.C., for my *quince*. There were so many paintings I'd wanted to see at the National Gallery and I really, really wanted to see the Museum of Women Artists. Ever since Mami had taken me to the Diego Rivera show and shown me a painting of Frida Kahlo, I had tried to learn all I could about women artists.

After school, I would go to the library and ask the librarian for books about Mary Cassatt, Faith Ringgold, and Elizabeth Catlett. But Frida Kahlo, with her elaborate Mexican costumes and her wild self-portraits, was my favorite.

"Let me see by a show of hands how many of you will be having *quinceañeras*."

Eight of the fifteen girls in the class raised their hands. I kept my hand half-raised. I looked around the room and one boy had his hand raised, too.

"Geronimo, are you having a *quinceañera*?" Mrs. Daniels asked, curiously.

"Not exactly," he said, shyly, looking at the other boys in the room. "It's just that I don't have any sisters and my mom really wants to do something fancy, so I'm having a big fifteenth birthday party. We're renting a hall and hiring a DJ. My cousin works at Hot 97, so we're trying to get Kid Capri to DJ my party."

Kid Capri was the hottest DJ in New York, and everyone was really impressed. Kids started calling out:

"Ooo, Geronimo, you know how close we are."

"Geronimo, *no me olvidas*."

"Do you need a date, Geronimo?"

Mrs. Daniels just laughed. "Okay, everybody, cool it. As you know, *quinceañeras* are the traditional coming-of-age party for young Latina girls. The fifteenth birthday symbolizes her passage from childhood into womanhood."

Magda threw up her hand.

"Mrs. Daniels, you're not Latina," she said. "How do

you know so much about *quinces?*"

"I did what any smart person does when they don't know something: I looked it up," Mrs. Daniels said, smiling. "I thought it would be fun, over the next couple of weeks, to spend our class studying not only *quinceañeras*, but different coming-of-age rituals. Can anyone name other coming-of-age rituals?"

Nobody raised their hands.

"When you're sixteen, you're allowed to drive," Geronimo called out. "I know because my mom's gonna get me a car."

"Show-off," Magda hissed.

"I guess that learning to drive can be considered a coming-of-age ritual. A very American one, at that. But I was thinking more of traditional ceremonies like the *quinceañera*."

I raised my hand.

"Well, in Judaism, they have bar mitzvahs and bat mitzvahs when you're thirteen."

"Yo, you get *a ton* of presents for that Jewish thing," said a boy named Eugene. "At my old school, I knew this Jewish kid and he invited me over to his house after he had that thing."

"It's called a bar mitzvah," Mrs. Daniels said.

"Yeah, that," Eugene said. "Homeboy cleaned up. Video games. Clothes. Model cars. Cash, too. Over a thousand dollars."

"So?" Marisa said. "I got money for my *quince*, too."

"Oh yeah?" said Eugene. "How much?"

"Okay, class, that's enough," Mrs. Daniels said. "This is a

history class, not an economics class. We're not here to talk about gifts. What we're going to do is talk about how different cultures celebrate coming of age. Got it?"

"Got it," we repeated.

"Good," she said. "Now in the Hopi tradition—"

"Hopi?" said Marisa. "What's that?"

"Class, does anyone know?"

I looked around the room, but nobody answered.

"Somebody guess," Mrs. Daniels said, encouragingly. "A good guess is better than no answer at all."

I raised my hand.

"The Hopi are a Native American tribe."

"Very good, Marisol," Mrs. Daniels said. "Now, do you know what the Hopi coming-of-age ritual is?"

I shook my head no.

"In the Hopi tradition, young women go into an underground area, called a kiva, where they carry out a secret initiation. As in many Native American cultures, this includes a traditional dance."

Magda raised her hand.

"Last year, in Panama, Marisol danced the *baile típico*. She wore a costume called a *pollera*. She didn't look American at all. It was really beautiful."

"Really, Marisol? That's wonderful," Mrs. Daniels said. "Maybe tomorrow, you'll tell the class all about it."

The bell rang and everyone piled out of the room.

"This is going to be fun, studying about *quinces* and other ceremonies in school," Magda said.

"Yeah, Mrs. Daniels rocks," I agreed. "Thanks for mentioning my dancing in Panama. That was sweet of you."

"Are you kidding? You looked so beautiful in your *pollera*. You were like a real Panamanian girl. I was kind of jealous, actually."

"Yeah, right."

I felt someone knock into me and I turned around.

"You think you're such a brainiac," Marisa said, standing two inches from my face. "The way you kiss up to the teacher—"

"Just leave it alone, Marisa," Magda warned.

"I'm not impressed, Miss Know-It-All," Marisa said, sailing past us. "I don't care what you did in Panama. You're just a nerd here."

I turned to Magda and put my hand on my hip.

"Tell me again. Why are you friends with her?"

"She's not that bad. Not most of the time."

"No, she's awful. *All the time*."

"I've got to have other friends, Marisol. You can't be my only friend."

I shrugged and swallowed a dozen words, each hanging like a pit in my throat. "Why can't I be your only friend?" I wanted to say. "Why isn't hanging out with me enough?"

After school, Magda and I took the bus out to the Kings Plaza mall. When we got to the store, Ann, the same saleswoman we'd seen the last time, was working.

"Hi, girls," she said, cheerfully.

"I'm here to pick up a dress," Magda said, reaching for the receipt. "It was being altered."

"I'll be right back," Ann said, as she disappeared into the storeroom.

"I'm so excited! I'm so excited!" Magda said. "I can hardly wait until I get the rest of my *quince* things. I've got to get a crown and flat shoes and high heels. Now that I've got my dress, I can pick out the dresses for the girls in my court. Even if you don't have a *quince*, you're still my *dama*. You don't have to wear the same dress as the other girls if you don't want to."

In the *quinceañera* court, the *quince's* best friend is called the *dama de honor*. It's sort of like being the maid of honor at a wedding.

"Okay," I mumbled, begrudingly.

"What are you going to do about your *quince*, girl?" Magda asked. "It's only four months away."

"I know. I know," I said, feeling my head start to pound. If I couldn't have the *quince* of my dreams, then I just wanted to forget all about it.

"Then you should have it at your Tía Alicia's. You could probably fit fifty people in that basement. You wouldn't have room for a court. But you don't really need one."

Magda's parents had reserved the Brooklyn Lodge, a private banquet hall, months ago. Her mother had invited more than a hundred people. They even had relatives coming in from Panama for her *quince*.

Ann returned with Magda's dress. "Here it is," she said, smiling. "Enjoy it."

"I will," Magda said, beaming. "I will."

As we walked through the Junior Formal section, I paused in front of my cranberry-red dress. I had about half the money saved for it. "I'll be back," I whispered as we walked past it.

"Let's go to the jewelry section," Magda said. "I want to see what kind of earrings would go with this dress."

"No problem."

At the first counter, a white-haired older woman gave us a look and said, "You don't want to look here, girls. These earrings are real gold and *very* expensive."

Magda flashed her rings at her and said, "That's fine, because my father is *very* rich. He's throwing me a big party for my eighteenth birthday. . . ."

I gave her a puzzled look. Eighteen? Didn't she mean fifteen?

Magda discreetly kicked me in the knee. "It's my eighteenth birthday," she continued. "And my father asked me to pick out a pair of earrings to go with the dress."

"Harrumph," the woman sniffed, looking doubtful. "Let me see the dress."

Magda showed it to her. The woman must have been suitably impressed because all of a sudden, her tone changed.

"It's a beautiful dress, and costs a pretty penny too," she said, fingering the price tag on the dress. "Now with a beautiful black dress, what you want to wear are diamonds."

She pulled out a black velvet tray of diamond earrings. "These are diamonds in a gold setting," she said, pointing with a perfectly manicured red fingernail. "These are diamonds in a platinum setting. But for a young woman like yourself, I'd recommend diamond studs."

Marisol must have spent half an hour trying on every pair of earrings at the counter. Finally, she said, "I can't decide. They're all so lovely, I just can't decide. I'll have to come back with Daddy. He'll choose. Do you have a card? I'd love for you to meet Daddy. You've been oh-so-helpful."

All I could do was stare. Magda played the spoiled-rich-girl routine to the hilt. The woman handed Magda her card and we walked out of the store. As we did, Magda threw the woman's card away.

"You are unbelievable!"

"Was I good?" she said, smiling.

"Good—you were excellent. 'I'll have to come back with Daddy. . . . You've been oh-so-helpful.' You've never called Tío Ricardo 'Daddy' in your whole life!"

Magda did impersonations of the saleswoman that were so funny, I'd thought I'd pee on the spot. When the bus arrived, we paid our fare, then headed toward our usual spot in the back.

"I'm a good actress, aren't I?" Magda asked.

"The *best*," I assured her.

"Well, I'm an even better thief," she said, producing a pair of diamond studs from her pocket.

"Magda, you didn't," I said, softly, backing away from her as I did. I looked up for a bolt of lightning to strike her down, but nothing happened. The bus rambled on.

"You didn't even see me," she said, grinning.

"Magda, you can't do this," I said, my voice trembling. "Those earrings are worth a fortune."

"They're mine now. And that saleswoman. Racist old bat. Do you see how she treated us when we first came to the counter? She deserves to be robbed."

"Magda . . ."

"Come on," she said. "Don't ruin it for me by getting all Goody Two-shoes."

"What are you going to tell your parents?"

"I'll tell them that Sammy bought them for me."

"They'll go for that?"

"My parents don't know real diamonds from fake diamonds. I'll tell them they're *fantasía*."

I thought back to the day in the hallway when Marisa was had worn her beautiful gold earrings.

"Is that what you do with Marisa?" I asked. "Steal earrings?"

"Earrings are easy to steal. They're small, light, and they don't have those big sensors clomped onto them."

"I'm not hearing this," I said, sitting with my head in my lap.

"Come on, Marisol. Get with the program. Do you want these?" she said, the diamonds glittering like icicles in her palm. "I'll just get another pair."

"I don't want them," I said, turning toward the window.

"Why?"

"Because they're stolen!" I yelled.

"Sssshhh," Magda said, pulling my arm so hard I thought it would come out of the socket. "Fine with me if you're going to be a total nerd. But don't get me busted."

I rang the bell and stood to get up.

"This isn't our stop," Magda said.

"I know. I'll walk the rest of the way home."

"Suit yourself," Magda said, giving me a dirty look.

"'Bye," I said as I stepped off of the bus. But she didn't say a word.

I walked through the cold December air, covering my ears with my gloved hands. I'd forgotten my hat on the bus. Damn. I couldn't believe Magda. Stealing lipstick was bad enough. Stealing diamonds—I couldn't even imagine it. The thing was is that she had so much. Tío Ricardo wasn't rich by any means, but he kept her in gold, new clothes, and designer sneakers. He'd been saving for her *quince* since the day she was born, practically. She had everything. Why was she acting so crazy?

12

By the time I got home from the mall, I had just enough time to drop off my books, change my clothes, and run over to Mrs. Trader's house to pick up Tyson.

I rang the doorbell and Mrs. Trader opened the door. She was dressed in a blue skirt with a matching jacket. She probably hadn't left the house all day, but Mrs. Trader always got dressed up. "Only sick or dying people spend all day in their pajamas," she would say.

She was almost eighty years old, but there was hardly a crease on her face. "Good black don't crack," she always said. In the old days, Mrs. Trader used to be a jazz singer. All around her house there were pictures of her with other people I didn't recognize, but Mrs. Trader assured me that they were all famous. Just as she had been once.

"How are you today, dear?" she asked, sweetly.

"Fine," I answered rotely.

"You don't seem fine," she said. "Would you like a cup of tea and a piece of my homemade pecan pie?"

"Okay," I said.

Mrs. Trader set a cup of tea and a piece of pie before me.

"I hear you're saving for a dress," she said. "A special dress."

"Who told you?"

"My friends next door. Luísa and Ricardo are very proud of how hard you work."

"Thank you. The dress is for my *quinceañera*."

"Luisa told me about those things. They're like Sweet Sixteen, but a year earlier."

"Exactly," I said, scarfing down the pie. "Did you have a Sweet Sixteen party?"

"Girl, it's a miracle I can even remember back that far. I didn't have a Sweet Sixteen, but I think it's a beautiful tradition. It's important that we show our girls that we care. That we see them becoming women and we want to help guide the way."

"What a cool way to put it."

"I try to be cool," Mrs. Trader said, winking at me.

I finished off the pie and licked the fork clean. "You make the *best* pecan pie, Mrs. Trader."

"Nothing but sugar and pecans in there."

"It's the absolute best," I said, feeding Tyson a little piece.

"Don't spoil the dog," Mrs. Trader said, shaking a finger at me. But I know she didn't mean it. She treated Tyson more like a son than a dog.

I put a leash on Tyson and looked at my watch: six-fifteen.

"My aunt is supposed to meet me here after I walk Tyson. Will you look out for her if I'm a little late?"

"Of course, dear," Mrs. Trader said. "Be careful out there."

I walked Tyson in the direction away from Magda's house and prayed that I wouldn't bump into her. Luckily, I didn't. When I got back, Tía China was sitting in Mrs. Trader's living room, eating pecan pie.

"This pie is *fabuloso*," Tía China said. I had to do a double take when I saw her. Her short blond hair was now long, dark, and straight.

"It's a wig," she said, answering the question before I could ask it. "And we better run. It's Alicia's wedding anniversary and they're going out to dinner. They probably have reservations, so we better not be late."

"*Gracias* for the pie," Tía China said, giving Mrs. Trader a kiss on the cheek. "Next time, you've got to sing for me."

"Oh, girl, please," Mrs. Trader said, playfully waving Tía China away. "Sing? I'd sing in the lounge of a Roach Motel. You don't have to ask me twice."

We said our good-byes and were on our way.

"Nice ride," I said as Tía China opened the passenger door of a brand-new convertible.

"I know," she said, grinning. "My new *novio* is a manager at the Plaza Hotel. I met him at a fashion show. He is the sweetest guy—with equally good taste in women and automobiles."

"Tía China . . ." I began. "If I tell you something, promise not to tell Mami."

"Promise," Tía China said, as she backed out of the parking space and drove to the corner.

"I mean it!" I said.

She turned to me and crossed her heart. "I promise."

"Magda's been shoplifting. She stole a pair of earrings today when we were at the mall."

"*Niña*, no. I can't believe it."

"*Diamond* earrings. Real ones."

She whistled. "Do you know what would have happened to you if you were caught?"

"But I didn't steal anything. I didn't even know about it until we were on the bus."

"Do you think the police would have cared? Shoplifters use accomplices all the time, to distract the salesperson while they steal."

I sat back, dumbfounded. *Accomplice* was such a funny word. The sort of thing you hear about on television cop shows. I never thought the word would apply to me.

"It's these girls she's been hanging out with, Marisa and Elizabeth. They shoplift all the time. I keep telling her that she should be careful, but she doesn't want to hear it. What should I do?"

"I guess there's nothing you can do, short of telling her parents. Then she'll hate you and they might not even believe you. You've just got to keep your distance that's all. And no matter what you do, you can't go to the mall with her. Don't go to any store of any kind with her. Do you hear me?"

"I understand. . . . Are you going to tell Mami?"

"No. But I think you should."

"Think again," I grumbled.

"Your choice," Tía China said, pulling into Tía Alicia's driveway. "I'm just telling you, *cuídate, niña*. Be careful."

I had to ring Tía Alicia's bell three times before she answered. When she did, she was wearing a navy wool dress with pink embroidered flowers and a huge smile.

I looked at my watch: seven-fifteen. *"Estoy tarde,"* I said. "I'm sorry to keep you waiting."

"No importa," Tía Alicia said, kissing me on a cheek and giving me a bear hug. She smelled, as usual, of roses with the faint smell of Agua de Florida underneath.

"China," she said, kissing my aunt on the cheek as well.

"I just need a few minutes to get ready," Tía Alicia said. "I'll be right back. Jason is in the basement, playing video games. *Tú sabes.*"

"I'll go play with him," I said. My little cousin Jason was one of my favorites.

I opened the basement door, but it was dark and strangely quiet at the bottom of the steps. Maybe Jason had heard me come in and was playing hide-and-seek.

"I know you're down there, Jason!" I called out from the top of the steps.

I reached for the flashlight Tía Alicia kept in a basket near the door and turned it on.

"Oh, Pepito!" I cooed. "Pepito Mala Pata!" Pepito Mala Pata was Spanish for Dennis the Menance. It was also Jason's nickname.

I heard the fluttering of little feet and I laughed.

"I'm gonna get you and when I do . . ."

All of a sudden, the basement lights flicked on. There must have been thirty people down there, yelling "Surprise!" all at once.

I screamed, then fell back onto a chair. Mami was standing at the center of the group. "Are you okay?"

"You-ss-cc-ared me!" I managed to spit out. "What's going on?"

"*Esta buena gente,*" Mami said, gesturing to the group of people. "These good people are your *quinceañera padrinos.*"

"*Padrinos?* Godparents?"

"For months I've been agonizing about how to throw you a *quince,*" Mami said. She put her arm around me as her eyes filled with tears. "Then Elsa Rivera suggested we do it the Mexican way, by asking different people to pay for a part of the ceremony."

"Wasn't that the best idea, Mari-boom?" Eduardo asked me. Mari-boom? *Where* did he get these names from?

Forget the names, where did Eduardo get his clothes? I couldn't believe the bright orange shirt he was wearing. For a second, I thought he might have gotten dressed in the dark, but a shirt like that would glow in the dark. He stood, glued to Mami's side, his arm slung around her shoulder. On any other day, his silly nicknames, bad fashion sense, and his acting so lovey-dovey with my *mami* would have gotten on my last nerve. But I was too blown away by the room full of fairy godmothers and fathers to do more than note all the annoying details about Eduardo and mentally file them away for future reference.

I looked around the room and saw a lot of familiar faces: my cousins Roxana and Manuel, the Vegas and the Molinas, people who had known Mami and the *tías* from back home, back in Panama. But there were a lot of strangers too, men and women I'd never laid eyes on before. What were they doing at a party for me?

"*Pero*, Mami," I whispered. "I don't even *know* some of these people."

I guess I didn't really whisper it, because a large man, with a belly out to *here*, came right up to me and said, "I know you don't know us. But we sure do know you, Marisol Mayaguez. Your *mami*'s been showing us your school pictures since the days when you barely had teeth to smile." And at that note, he pulled out a picture of me from the second grade. Folks started to gather, all looking at the goofy picture of me with lopsided pigtails and more spaces than teeth in my mouth.

"Hey!" I said, reaching for the picture. "How'd you get that?"

"Inez gave it to me," the man said, cheerfully. "And you can't have it, because it's mine. By the way, my name is Dr. Christopher July and I'm the *padrino* of the flowers. My wife's a florist and she's already excited about showing you the bouquet she wants to make for you, as well as what she has in mind for the table arrangements."

My head was spinning. A bouquet? Table arrangements? Was I dreaming?

Dr. July handed me an envelope. "This is just a token of my promise," he said.

I opened it; it was a *quinceañera* card from my new *padrinos:* Dr. and Mrs. July.

Mami gave Dr. July a hug and thanked him for coming.

"I've got to run," he said to me, extending a hand for me to shake. "Evening rounds. But I will see you on May first. Save me a dance, okay?"

I nodded, stunned.

"Marisol, say something!" Mami hissed.

"Nice to meet you," I said, in a robotlike voice.

"Nice to meet you, too," Dr. July said. He turned then to Mami and said, "Don't worry about her manners. She's just a litle shocked, that's all."

"You don't know me either, Marisol," said a short, sassy woman with a long salt-and-pepper braid down her back. "I'm Lilian Gomez. I'm the *madrina* of the invitations."

"*Mucho gusto.* Pleased to meet you," I said, rising to give her a kiss on the cheek. "And thank you."

"*Dame un besito, también,*" said a young woman with olive-colored skin and black hair tied into a bun. She pointed to her cheek and I gave her a kiss. "I'm Elsa Rivera, and this was my idea!"

Mami threw her arm around Miss Rivera. "Oh, Elsa," she laughed. "Nobody was going to forget you."

"You better not," Miss Rivera said, giving me a wink. "I am also a *madrina* and I will be providing the last doll."

I was confused. "But I don't play with dolls!"

Miss Rivera turned to Mami and said. "*No me digas!* Don't tell me she doesn't know about the last doll! The last doll is what you bring into the church during your *quinceañera misa*. You give your *mami* the doll and she will give you a new rosary and bible. It symbolizes your leaving behind childish things."

"Wow," I said in awe. The very phrase, "leaving behind childish things," sent a chill down my spine.

"I guess you never saw Lily's last doll," Mami explained, "because we didn't go to her *quince* church service, just the party afterward."

Speaking of which, in Tía Alicia's basement, a party was in full swing. It was only a Wednesday night, but they had put on some slamming salsa tracks, and on the buffet table there was an assortment of food: *arroz con camarones, plátanos maduros,* stewed chicken. People were milling about and talking, but I was still plopped in the same chair that I'd fallen back on when I first came in.

My little *primo* Jason brought me a cup of Tía Alicia's ginger fruit punch.

"*Gracias*, Jason," I said, giving him a kiss on the cheek. "Did you know about this?"

"Yes, Marisol," he said. He was six years old, but short for his age. He had a little Afro and was already in his pajamas. "But I didn't say a word. You came looking for me with a flashlight, too!"

"You bet I did!" I said. "I thought we were going to play video games, Pepito Mala Pata."

"Ooo! Marisol, *ven acá*," Jason said, trying to pull me from my chair. "Let's go play now."

"Not now," Mami said. "Marisol has to talk to all of her *padrinos*."

"But Marisol always plays with me!" Jason said.

"Jason, *no voy a decirte dos veces!*" Mami said in a stern voice and Jason slunk away.

Celia and Alfredo Molina came over with their daughter, Kiki.

"*Buenas*," they said, as they each hugged me. "How's our favorite baby-sitter?"

"Good!" I beamed. "How you doing, Kiki?"

"Hi, Marisol," Kiki said, shyly hanging on to her father's pant leg. "Please, make me a sandwich, please?"

Everyone laughed.

"In a few minutes, okay?" I asked, gesturing for her to come sit on my lap.

"She's not hungry! We just ate," Mr. Molina said. "Don't you have something to give Marisol, Kiki?"

Kiki handed me a red envelope.

"*Gracias*," I said, putting the envelope to my heart. I opened it and almost fainted. "Mami, the Molinas are going to be the *padrinos* of the banquet hall. They're renting me the Brooklyn Lodge!"

I'd passed the Brooklyn Lodge, a million times, on the way to Tía Alicia's. From the outside, it was a stately and elegant brick building with a display window near the front door announcing the week's events. I'd never been inside. Magda's sister, Evelyn, had gone to a wedding there, and she said it was amazing; that it had fountains and a waterfall along one wall in the main dining room.

Mami kissed Mr. and Mrs. Molina. "Thank you both so much," she said. "You know the Orchard Beach Community Center would have been just fine. I really don't want anyone to overextend themselves."

"*No te preocupes*. I know when the time comes, you'll be helping us throw a *quince* for Kiki," Mr. Molina said, scooping his daughter up in his arms.

"*Claro qué sí*, Alfredo," Mami said. "We'll be there for Kiki. Even Marisol will be old enough to be the *madrina* of something. But you never told me. How did you manage to get the Brooklyn Lodge?"

"One of the partners in my law firm is an investor, and when I told him that Marisol was like a second daughter to me, he offered it to me at cost. Of course, we're going to have to have Marisol's *quince* on Monday morning at ten . . ."

Mrs. Molina jokingly punched Mr. Molina on the arm. "You better stop it, Alfredo. . . ."

"Marisol won't mind having her *quince* on a Monday morning, will she?" Mr. Molina teased.

"No, not at all," I said, looking up, my eyes wet with tears. Whenever I heard grown-ups talk about tears of happiness, I always thought it sounded so stupid. But looking around at all these people who'd come together to make my *quince* dreams come true. I knew then, that for the first time, I, too, was crying tears of joy. It was as if my heart was a river, overflowing.

"Oh no, she's started crying," Mr. Molina said, throwing up his arms and smiling broadly. "What is it with the women and the tears?"

He handed me his handkerchief.

I pressed the perfectly ironed white triangle to each eye. Then I rubbed a finger over the blue embroidered letters: ALM—Alfredo Luis Molina. ALM: one more A and it would spell *alma*, which means "soul."

Mami knelt next to my chair and hugged me tight. "I know, *niña*. It's overwhelming."

She was right. It was overwhelming. But the thing that really got to me was when Mr. Molina said I was like a second daughter to him. He'd never said that before. It made me think of my *papi*. I missed him the worst at times like this. Missing Papi made me cry, but it was Mami and the *tías* and friends like the Molinas who filled my *alma*, who kept my spirit strong.

"Marisol," Kiki said, tugging on my sleeve. "Can I be a *dama* in your *quince*?"

Tía China came over and put her hands on her hips. "Little Kiki, what do you know about being a *dama*?"

"My Mami told me that Marisol is going to wear a dress like a princess and that her best friends will get to wear princess dresses, too. Mami said that the other girls are called *damas*."

"Kiki you're too small to be a *dama*. . . ." I began, but Mami interrupted.

"You know what, Kiki?" Mami said. "I have an idea of how you could be in Marisol's *quince*."

Then she linked arms with Mrs. Molina. "*Venga*, Celia. Let's take a little walk."

The two of them walked away, but from the corner I heard Mrs. Molina say, "That's the *perfect* idea." And I wondered what they were cooking up.

My *tías* appeared before me: Tía Julia, Tía Alicia, Tía China.

Tía China straightened out my braids and said, "Needless to say, I will be the *madrina* of the crazy cool hairstyle."

Tía Julia scowled. "Not crazy."

Tía Alicia chimed in. "Not even cool. Not for the *quince*. It must be traditional and beautiful."

"We'll see," Tía China said, raising her left eyebrow at her older sisters. "But I will also be the *madrina* of music. I'm in charge of hiring the DJ. *Wepa, loca!*"

"*Un mil gracias*," I said, giving Tía China a hug. "Now I know the music is going to be bangin'."

Then we turned to each other and started singing, "*Boricua. Moreno.*"

Tío Diego came by and said, "Hey, don't forget *los viejos*. It won't be a true *quinceañera* without Panamanian classics like "La Parada." I've got them all on LP. . . ."

"I know you do, Tío," I said, squeezing his hand. "We'll do a little *pasito* for the old folks, too."

Everybody laughed.

Then, Tía Alicia and Tía Julia handed me a card. It was a beautiful mint green with ink-black lettering like calligraphy. I recognized the beautiful handwriting as Tía Alicia's. "We are providing the catering and a beautiful cake for our most precious niece's *quince*." The note was signed: "*Con carinos*, Tía Alicia and Tía Julia."

"*Gracias, tías*," I said, giving them each a *besito* on the cheek.

"We're so proud of you," Tía Julia said. She was dressed in a dark blue business suit. Of all my aunts, she was the most somber. "You are growing up to be a fine young lady."

A fine young lady? I flashed to the incident earlier in the day with Magda and the diamond earrings. If Magda had gotten caught . . . If I had been arrested, as an accomplice . . . My *tías* wouldn't have thought such good things about me. And worse! I could have been sitting in a police station instead of at a party with all my *quince padrinos*.

Eduardo and Mami came over, holding hands. He handed me an envelope. Inside was a glittery picture of a crown. There are five traditional *quince* gifts: a bible, earrings, a medal, a bracelet and a crown. Each item is meant to reinforce the *quinceañera's* faith in God. The earrings remind her to listen to God's word. The medal is a symbol of her piety.

The bracelet is the unbroken circle of God's love, and the crown designates her as a queen before God.

"If you don't mind, Mari, I'll be the *padrino* of your crown," Eduardo said. Then he turned to Mami, gazing at her lovingly. "Inez, you don't need a crown for the world to know that you're a queen."

"*Ay, cariño,*" Mami said, giving Eduardo a hug.

"*Gracias*, Eduardo," I said, looking up at him. "I can't wait to see my crown."

In my mind, I flashed back to the part of Lily's *quince* when her father changed her shoes from flats to heels to symbolize her walk into womanhood. Who would buy my heels? Who would change my shoes? Would I have to ask Eduardo? Would Tío Ricardo do it?

Mami brought over an older black woman with impossibly smooth skin and short, silver-colored hair.

"I'm Mrs. Dove," the woman said. "I'm going to be the godmother of your limousine."

"Limousine?" I repeated. Now I knew I was dreaming.

"Somebody wake me up, please," I begged.

Mami just smiled.

"I've worked with Inez for years and I've heard so much about you." Mrs. Dove pulled a wrinkled piece of paper out of her handbag. It was the certificate I got for reading the most books in the fifth-grade reading contest.

"I can't believe you have that!"

"Believe it. You're no stranger to me, Marisol Mayaguez. And I'm happy to be part of the festivities," Mrs. Dove said.

"My husband drives a limo for all those fancy Wall Street types. As your fifteenth birthday present, he's going to pick you up, drive you to your party, then pick you up when the party's over."

"A limousine . . ." I repeated, dazed.

"This isn't a professional, medical opinion," Mrs. Dove said, winking at me. "But I really would have her ears checked."

I got up and gave Mrs. Dove a kiss. "Thank you. It's not enough, but I don't know how else to thank you."

"Continue being a good kid," Mrs. Dove said. "Go to college. I didn't know about this fifteenth-birthday tradition, but I think it's wonderful for the community to come together to honor young girls and guide them into womanhood."

Tía China told me that in some parts of the country, priests were against *quinces*. The priests thought they encouraged girls to have sex too early. I thought about the girl Junior Vasquez was supposed to have gotten pregnant and the talk that I heard from girls around school. A lot of kids at my school were having sex, or at least thinking about it. *Quinces* didn't have anything to do with it.

Then Tía China came down the steps holding a familiar-looking garment bag. I looked at it and then looked away. It couldn't be.

She brought it to me and laid it across my lap.

"It's from Mrs. Trader," Tía China said. "Also, Ann at the store told me to tell you hello and happy *quinceañera*."

I opened the card taped to the garment bag, and

recognized Mrs. Trader's small, loopy handwriting. The note said, simply: "Shine, baby. Shine."

I started to unzip the bag, and when I saw the cranberry-red satin fall like a pile of feathers onto my lap, I felt the tears coming again.

"Hey, hey, careful," Mr. Molina said, jokingly. "No crying on the dress. We can't return it if it's all *mojada*."

The whole room laughed. Someone put on Tito Puente and the room filled with pulsating rhythms.

"*Baile conmigo?*" Eduardo asked Mami, bowing formally like an old-fashioned *caballero*.

"*Con gusto,*" Mami said.

They began to dance, and despite the fast music, Eduardo and Mami danced slow and close. Mami liked him, I could tell. I guess I was going to have to get used to him. But he was going to have to learn my name. It was Marisol. Not Marisolita. Not Mari. I looked down at the dress in my lap, then looked over again at Eduardo. I'd deal with him and his nicknames another night. Tonight, everything was perfect.

Elsa Rivera and Tía China were rattling in Spanglish about boyfriends, eyebrow waxing, and the pros and cons of going to Club Med on your honeymoon.

"Honeymoon?" I asked, rolling my eyes. "You've been going out with that guy for two weeks!"

"*Si no él, será otro!*" Tía China said, flirtatiously. "Speaking of which, who's going to be your *caballero* at the *quince*?"

A date? I'd been so preoccupied with the money, I didn't even think about a date.

"I don't know!" I told Tía China and Mami's friend, Elsa.

"So many *quince* details! So little time!" Elsa said, giving me a nudge and a smile.

I looked around and saw that Kiki and Jason were playing video games. Lilian Gomez was talking to Tía Alicia about what kind of fish she liked to use in her *tostados de pescado*. Mrs. Dove and the Molinas were chatting about eco-tourism in Panama. My cousin Roxana was in the corner making googy-eyes at one of the young interns that Eduardo had brought to the party. Sitting in Tía Alicia's basement, surrounded by a roomful of *padrinos* clucking in English and Spanish, it made me think of a poem I had learned in school. The poem was called "English *con salsa*" and it was by a writer named Gina Valdes:

> Welcome to ESL 100, English Surely Latinized. . . .
> We speak English *refrito*, English *con sal y limón*,
> English thick as mango juice, English poured from
> a clay jug . . . English with a red cactus
> flower blooming in its heart.

That was me: an American-born Panamanian girl about to have her *quince*. With Magda I spoke English *refrito*. With Mami and my *tías*, I spoke English *con sal y limón*. And now, looking around the room at all of the people who had given me so much, I could feel the *flores* blooming in my heart.

13

Usually, I had no trouble paying attention in Spanish class. It was one of my favorite classes. My teacher, Luisa Fernandez, was tall and elegant with straight black hair cut into a bob and flawless *café au lait* skin. When I'd first walked into class, I was surprised to see that Mrs. Fernandez was Chinese, but as she explained, she was China-Latina; her family had grown up in Cuba. Mrs. Fernandez was cool. She was always bringing in different things to help us understand Spanish. One day, she showed us slides of paintings from El Prado, the famous museum in Spain. My favorite was a painting called *Las Meninas*, in which the painter, a guy named Velasquez, had painted a picture of himself with a palette and the paintbrushes while the beautiful princess posed.

This week, we were studying poems by Martin Espada, the Puerto Rican poet. My copy of Espada's book, *Rebellion is the Circle of a Lover's Hand*, lay open on my desk. I love poetry, but today my mind was on other things—Mami, her *novio*, my *quinceañera* dress. I couldn't wait for lunch time to tell Magda about my *padrinos* and how I was really going to have my own *quince*, at the Brooklyn Lodge, of all places!

"Señorita Mayaguez," Mrs. Fernandez called out. "What does Martin Espada mean when he says '*los españoles conquistaron con hierro y palabras*'?"

"The Spanish conquered with iron and words?" I repeated, fumbling for my book, but I wasn't even on the right page.

"We're reading 'Colibri.'"

"*Discúlpame,* Señora Fernandez," I said, contritely. "I wasn't paying attention."

"We're on page thirty-four," Señora Fernandez said, generously.

I turned to the right page and thought for a moment, twisting a strand of my hair. "I think what Señor Espada is saying is that when the Spanish conquered Latin America it wasn't just with weapons. The Spaniards had a sense of entitlement, they came in with fancy words and classified the native people with words that were deceiving and degrading."

Señora Fernandez smiled. "Very good, *señorita*. Now, *por favor, tratas a dar nosotros su atención*. Poetry can be almost as interesting as daydreaming, don't you think?"

I smiled, shyly. But everyone else in the class laughed. I was the only freshman in Spanish 3: Latin American Literature. Everybody else was a junior. I knew my Spanish was as good as theirs, if not better. Sometimes I felt intimidated because they were all older than I was. Magda, miraculously, had managed to fail Spanish 1 while I was away and was taking it again for the second year in a row.

When the bell rang, I threw my books into my knapsack, anxious to catch up with Magda *por una buena charla*. Then I saw that there was someone standing by my desk.

"Marisol, *qué tal?*" said Francisco, a tall, skinny junior who I'd seen, but never talked to before. He was cute, with a shaved head like a basketball player and dark, creamy skin. Self-consciously, I scratched the pimple on my cheek.

"Hey, Francisco," I said, "what's up?"

"Nice save about Martin Espada and those awful *conquistadores*," he said, smiling.

"Thanks."

"I love the last line of that poem," Francisco said, taking my hand and examining it. "*Si la historia solo fuera como tus manos*. If only history were like your hands."

"Oh yeah, I like that line, too," I said, pulling my hand away and fumbling with the handle on my bag. "I felt like such a goofball in class today. I didn't even know what page we were on."

"It doesn't matter, Señora Fernandez knows that you're the best student in the class," Francisco said, flatteringly. "Is it really true that you're only a freshman?"

"Only a freshman?" I said, mischievously. "Yes, I'm *only* a freshman, which makes me the lowest of the low. But somehow I manage to drag myself out of bed every day."

"Come on, that's not what I meant," he said, blushing. "I just meant your Spanish is really, really good."

"I spent last year going to school in Panama," I explained.

"You're Panamanian?" Francisco said, grinning. "So am I."

"I'm surprised that our parents don't know each other," I said. "My mother seems to know every other Panamanian in New York. Where are your folks from?"

"Balboa," he said.

"Oh, we're from Panama City," I said, surprising myself by the way I had said "we." I used to say, "My mother's from Panama City." But now that I'd been there, now that I knew what it was like to clean my shoes with leaves from the hybrid tree, and what it felt like to drink *agua de pipa* straight from the coconut gourd. I felt like I was from Panama City too.

I remembered then that I was supposed to meet Magda in the lunchroom. "I better go," I said, standing up. "I'm supposed to meet my friend."

"Well, it was nice talking to you," Francisco said. "See you around."

"Yeah, *hasta la próxima,*" I said, smiling. Then I turned the corner and booked for the lunchroom.

When I got downstairs, Magda was nowhere in sight. I

went through the lunch line, trying to decide which was the lesser evil: pizza with some sort of atomic-looking cheese or a hamburger with some very questionable meat. I took the pizza, filled my cup with Coke, and paid for my purchases.

My eyes swept through the room again, looking for Magdalena. But I didn't see her. Now I had even more stuff to tell her. Not only was I having a *quince,* but Francisco had spoken to me. I had flirted with him. I didn't even know I knew how! I thought then of Rubén, back in Panama. I had cried when I said good-bye to him, that last day, in front of Abuela's house. We'd promised to write, but sometime over the summer, the letters stopped coming. *Mi amiga* Ana had written to say that she could tell he missed me, that he didn't have a new *novia.* But I still felt sad. I wondered if having a boyfriend was just one more magical thing that had happened in Panama, but wouldn't happen when I got back home. Now I'd met Francisco and he seemed to like me. I wondered if, somehow, I hadn't brought some of that Panama magic back home with me after all.

I had already finished my lunch and was circling things in the latest dELiA catalog when Magda's friends Marisa and Elizabeth sat down.

"Elizabeth, I forgot to get a straw. . . ." Marisa said, pouting. Whenever she wanted something, she turned on this fake sweet voice that made me sick.

"Here, take my straw," Elizabeth said, jumping to her feet. "I'll go get another one."

"Thank you *so much,*" Marisa said, adding a little punch to each word like the cheerleader she was.

"Where's Magda?" I asked.

"She had to do a make-up test in algebra," she said. "We all did because we cut class last Friday afternoon."

"Why'd you cut class?" I asked, wondering why Magda hadn't mentioned anything to me.

"Shopping," Marisa said.

"Yeah, lots of shopping," Elizabeth said, giggling as she sat back down. "You should come with us. Get down with the five-finger discount."

I grimaced, thinking about Magda and the diamond earrings she'd helped herself to the day before.

"Why are you always circling things in catalogs when you never buy anything?" Marisa said, snatching the dELiA catalog out of my hand.

"Hey, give that back," I said, embarrassed. I didn't think anybody had noticed the way I circled things in catalogs. Even if I couldn't buy much, I liked to pick out the stuff I liked. What business was it of Marisa's?

"Rosette handbag?" Marisa zoomed in on the first circled item. "For what? To carry around your government handouts?"

"Give it back," I said evenly.

Marisa flipped through until she came to the next dog-eared page. "Leather loafers," she read, giggling. "Air Max sneakers. Satin pumps. The notion that you could afford any of this is truly hilarious. You know, Marisol, you should be a comedian."

"Keep the catalog, Marisa," I said, opening my book of Martin Espada poetry. I scanned the dining room for Magda. Where the hell was she? I was about to go postal on her friend.

"Crewneck cashmere sweater," Marisa read out. "In cornflower blue and charcoal gray."

I could feel my face getting hot and I reached again for the catalog.

"Now, Marisol," Marisa said condescendingly. "In which lifetime will you ever be able to afford one, let alone, two cashmere sweaters?"

I looked around the room nervously, wondering if anyone could hear Marisa dissing me, but it was late and the lunch crowd was thinning out. I glanced again at the door. I wanted to wait for Magda to talk to her about all the people who were going to be the godparents of my *quince* and about Francisco, a bona-fide junior, talking to me after class. But lunch was almost over.

"Marisa, let's not do this," I said, my breath heavy as I snatched the catalog back. "Just mind your business, because you have no idea what I can and can't afford."

"That's where you're wrong, because I think I do," Marisa snarled. "You wear the same pair of jeans to school every day. That is, when you're not wearing those khaki cargo pants. And how many times a week do you think you can wear that pathetic little blue dress that makes you look like a boat person?"

I felt like I'd been slapped. At the same time, I wanted to

ball up my fist and punch Marisa in the face. I'd had it with her crap. But instead of kicking her butt the way I wanted to, I did what I always do when I get mad—I cried.

"My—grandmother—made—me—that—dress—" I said, through my tears. Each word was a struggle, like a boulder being pushed up through my throat.

"That's exactly what it looks like. Like some tacky dress that your grandmother made," Marisa said, smugly. "I wouldn't advertise that if I were you."

She was wrong. The dress was made out of two beautiful blue swatches of material: one was a blue so pale, it looked like a raindrop. The other was aqua, blue like the two oceans that ran along either side of Panama. When my *abuela* had come home from the fabric shop with the material, she had laid them against my chest and smiled at how beautifully the colors complimented my cocoa-brown skin.

"The material is a little like your name," Abuela had said. "But instead of *mar y sol,* the sea and the sun, this dress will be the colors of *mar y cielo,* the sea and the sky."

Every time I wore that dress, I thought of my grandmother and how she taught me that I didn't need to have been born in Panama to be a true Panamanian. I carried the meaning of my family and our country in everything: in my name, in my clothes, in my heart.

"Everything has a meaning even if you don't know what it is," Abuela had said.

I grabbed my bag and started to walk away from the table, leaving my lunch tray behind me.

"Where you off to?" Marisa called out behind me. "Is the Salvation Army having a special on *quince* dresses?"

I didn't even look back. On the way out the door, I felt someone pull at my arm.

"What?" I said, spinning around. It was Magda. She was wearing a black turtleneck and a red plaid skirt. She had her hair pulled up in a ponytail and I couldn't help but notice the diamond studs glistening in her ears.

"Yo, calm down," she said. "What's going on?"

"Nothing," I said, wiping the tears from my eyes. "Ask your *friends.*"

"What are you talking about?" Magda said.

"Ma-r-r-r-isa and Eliz-z-z-abeth," I stammered, heading toward my locker. Magda followed me.

I opened my locker door and grabbed my history book.

"What did they say?" she asked.

"They laughed about the fact that I never have any money to order the clothes I circle in the dELiA catalog."

"So what do you care?"

"Marisa made fun of the dress my grandmother made me."

"The blue one?" Magda asked.

"Yes," I sniffed.

"Come on, Marisol. You know that's an old-school dress."

"I love that dress!"

"Okay, okay."

I turned to Magda and put my hand on her shoulder. "Marisa also told me about the five-finger discount you've been helping yourself to," I chastised. "You better watch out, Magda. Those girls are trouble."

"Are you lecturing me?" she asked, tapping a row of perfectly oval hot-pink fingernails against her black sweater.

"I'm not lecturing you," I said, sighing. "I'm just trying to give you some advice."

"Well, *thanks*," she said, her voice dripping with sarcasm. "And here's some advice for you. Don't cry so easily. It makes you look like a baby."

My mouth dropped and I tried to think of a clever comeback. But Magda had already begun to walk away. I thought about going after her, then decided against it. She was probably going to look for Elizabeth and Marisa, her new best friends.

I looked at the picture of me and Magda vamping in our bikinis that I'd taped to the inside of my locker door. I hadn't even gotten a chance to tell her about Francisco or my *quince*.

"What's going on with us?" I murmured to the girl in the picture, the one who I used to call my best friend. "*Nosotras vamos a pique*." Then the late bell rang and I hoisted my knapsack onto my shoulder, slamming the locker door shut.

14

The next morning I waited for Magda in front of the Rite Aid pharmacy, but she never showed. I looked down the corner and even walked to the traffic light on her block, but there was no sign of her. No matter how much we'd squabbled before, we *always* rode to school together. As I walked down to the subway station, I knelt to tie my shoelaces and self-consciously wiped a smudge off my sneakers. I would have loved a new pair of Air Maxes. Maybe now that Mrs. Trader had bought my *quince* dress, I could use my baby-sitting money to buy some new sneaks.

I was so late for school that I had no problem finding a seat on the train. I flipped through my *quinceañera* notebook of dreams and pulled out my favorite purple pen. Next to each page, I wrote in the name of my new *quinceañera* godmothers and godfathers. On the page that began the section on *quinceañera* dresses, I wrote "Mrs. Trader, *madrina* of the dress." On the page on which I had pasted pictures of different flowers, I wrote, "Dr. and Mrs. July, *padrinos* of the floral arrangements." Next to the pictures of *quinceañera* crowns, I wrote simply "Eduardo." I couldn't call him godfather, I couldn't call him anything with the word father in it, not yet.

When I got to homeroom, I saw Magda sitting in the back row with Marisa and Elizabeth. I smiled and waved, but she looked right through me. When the bell rang, I went right up to her and said, "Look, we need to talk."

Marisa just rolled her eyes at me, but Magda shooed her away.

"Talk about what?" she asked me, one hand on her hip.

"I'm sorry if I offended you yesterday, I was just so upset about Marisa."

"Look, I'm tired, okay? I'm tired of you dissing my friends. . . ."

I couldn't believe what I was hearing! "She dissed me first!"

"I'm tired of you acting like a Goody Two-shoes when we go shopping. . . ."

"Magda!"

"I offered you a gift and you threw it right back in my face."

"But Magda," I whispered, looking around the empty

classroom. "Those earrings were stolen!"

"See? That's what I mean. You're so judgmental. You used to be cool, but now . . ."

The late bell rang and Magda picked up her knapsack and started to walk away.

"Can we meet at lunch to talk about it?"

"Marisol, to tell you the truth, I don't think we have anything to talk about."

I followed her out into the hall and grabbed a hold of her sweater. "But I'm going to have a *quince*."

"Great. Welcome to the club."

"My mother found all these people to get me everything I need. There was a party."

"So I heard," Magda said, blithely.

"Aren't you going to be in my *quince*? You're supposed to be my *dama de honor*."

"I'll think about it."

She would think about it? *Mi mejor amiga?* My very best friend?

"Okay, Magda. Whatever." I turned to walk away. I almost started to cry, but then I thought of Magda's stinging words. She was right. I shouldn't cry so much. It made me look like a baby. I wiped the tears welling up in my eyes and ran to my algebra class.

When the lunch bell rang after Spanish class, I didn't know what to do. I couldn't bear the thought of walking into the cafeteria and seeing Marisa and Elizabeth. I started to walk toward the library, when I heard someone call my name. I turned and saw Francisco.

"Hey, Marisol. You're not going to lunch?"

"Well, um," I started to explain about Magda and Marisa, then I thought better of it. "I was just going to pick up a book from the library."

"Pick it up, later," Francisco said. "Come eat lunch with me."

I walked down the hall with him and tapped the little gold cross around my neck. Thank God for *milagritos*, as Mami would say.

"Nice sweater," I said, admiring his camel-colored turtleneck and the way it offset his beautiful dark skin.

"Thanks," he said, looking down at the sweater as if he'd never seen it before. "It was a Christmas present from my aunt."

We went through the lunch line, grimacing at the mangled Jell-O and the mystery meat that was being served in the hot tray. "I think the only safe bet is a sandwich," I said.

"I think you're right," Francisco agreed.

"Tuna fish or chicken salad?" I asked, holding one of each in my hands.

"Tuna," Francisco said.

We found a table near the window. As I sat down, I glanced over at where Magda sat. She looked at me and turned away. Marisa and Elizabeth did the same.

"Would you rather sit with your friends?" Francisco asked.

"No, it's okay," I muttered, unwrapping my sandwich.

"So tell me about yourself, Marisol Mayaguez."

It was such a line that I couldn't help but laugh.

"What do you want to know?" I teased, smiling for the first time all day.

We spent the whole lunch hour talking and joking. I learned that Francisco lived in Park Slope and had two little brothers. I told him about Mami and the year I spent in Panama. I also told him about my *quinceañera*. When the bell rang, we had made a date to go to the Museo Del Barrio in the Bronx. I'd never been, but Francisco had cousins in the Bronx and he went up there all the time. If Mami said okay, and she just had to say okay, we would go to the museum on Saturday afternoon.

When I got home from school, the house seemed so empty, the way it used to feel when Mami worked all day and went to school at night. Since Mami had finished her master's program, she hardly ever worked nights anymore. I was so proud of her. Sometimes I thought, maybe when I finished college, I would get a master's, too.

I sat at the dining room table with a cup of cocoa and a peanut-butter-and-banana sandwich. I laughed as I ate the sandwich. The influence that little Kiki was having on my eating habits was just ridiculous!

I struggled through the math homework. *Qué rompecabezas!* Then I took out the box of stationery that Mami kept in the kitchen drawer. I fired up my purple pen and wrote thank-you notes to all of the people who had agreed to sponsor my *quince*. It was a dream. All of it, except for the fact that Magda wasn't talking to me. Tía China was always saying that's just the way life was, always the rough and the smooth. I realized I had never really known what she meant until that moment.

I looked at my watch, then jumped out of my chair: 5:45. If I left right away, I would be just in time to walk Tyson. I grabbed my coat, locked the door to the apartment, and ran over to Mrs. Trader's.

I stopped at the corner deli and picked up a bouquet of daisies for Mrs. Trader. I was late, but hopefully she wouldn't mind. I walked past Marisol's house and paused for a second. Maybe I should try to talk to her, one last time. I'd go over after I walked Tyson.

I held the flowers behind my back and rang Mrs. Trader's bell.

"Good afternoon, dear," she said as she opened the door.

I gave her the flowers, then kissed her on the cheek. "Thank you for the dress! I couldn't believe it. How'd you know? It was such a surprise."

Mrs. Trader laughed. "That's what being a young woman should be about. Beautiful dresses, parties, and surprises."

"Will you come to my *quince?*"

"Wouldn't miss it for the world."

Tyson rolled around on the floor, flopping his tail from side to side.

"You're not invited, Ty," I teased, rubbing his belly.

"You better take him out," Mrs. Trader said. "I'll put these beautiful flowers in some water. Will you have some pie when you get back?"

"You don't have to ask me twice," I said. Then I put the leash around Tyson's neck and walked him to the door.

I walked him down to the Brooklyn College campus then around the block and back up Ocean Avenue. We were halfway down Foster Avenue when I saw Magda and Sammy Baldonado walking along, holding hands. I walked up to them.

"Hey, Marisol," Sammy said. "This must be Tyson. What's up, money?" He playfully put his hand around Tyson's muzzle, and the dog jumped up.

"Hey, Magda, what's up?" I asked.

"Not much," she said, looking away.

"I was thinking about coming over after I drop off Tyson."

"Sammy's coming over," Magda said, staring intently at the blinking sign in the liquor store across the street.

"Oh, okay," I said. "See you later."

"Catch you later, Marisol," Sammy said.

Magda didn't say a word. It was official. She was through with me.

Back at the house, Mrs. Trader and I sat down to a plate of blueberry pie and a cup of cocoa. Tyson cooled out by the fireplace. An old jazz record played on the stereo.

"Is that you singing?" I asked.

"Girl, I wish it was," Mrs. Trader said as she delicately cut a piece of pie. "But that is the one and only Dinah Washington."

"I like her voice."

" 'Was it in Tahiti,' " Mrs. Trader sang along. " 'Or was it on the Nile? Long ago, an hour or so, I recall, I saw you smile. . . . And I remember you. You're the one who made my dreams come true. A kiss or two ago.' "

I sat there, mesmerized by her voice and the romantic lyrics in the song. Then I had the most amazing idea.

"Mrs. Trader! Will you sing at my *quince?*"

"Well, I don't know," she said, coyly.

"Please!"

"Well, since you're being so insistent," she said, pursing her red lips. "I'd love to. What should I sing?"

For the next hour or so, Mrs. Trader played her favorite jazz tunes for me. We listened to Ella Fitzgerald and June Christy and Billie Holiday. I especially loved "God Bless the Child." It made me think of Mami and how hard she must have worked to bring all of those godparents together for me to have a *quince*. I knew I had to thank God for my *quince*, but I had to thank Mami, too.

"Can I call my *mami* and tell her where I'm at?"

"Of course, baby," Mrs. Trader said.

I called Mami and told her that I'd be home soon.

"No problem, *niña*," she said.

"Mrs. Trader said she would sing at my *quince*."

"That's a great idea," Mami agreed. "I'll see you soon.

Leave now, because it's getting dark. *Cuídate.*"

"I will, Mami."

I asked Mrs. Trader for a piece of pie to take home to Mami, and she gave me the whole thing. "I ain't got a thing to do but bake pies all day," she said, wrapping the pie in aluminum foil.

I knew she had kids and grandkids because I saw their pictures on the piano. Yet I wondered why she never visited them and why they never seemed to come to see her. But that was a question for another day.

"*Gracias*, Mrs. Trader," I said, giving her a *besito* on the cheek. "See you tomorrow."

"Good night, child," she said as she hugged me back.

I let myself into the apartment with my own key and was thrilled to find Mami putting the finishing touches on the dish she called "One Pot." Shrimp, codfish, sausages, olives, and rice simmered in a cast-iron pot on the stove.

"Hmmm, my favorite," I said. "Look, I brought dessert from Mrs. Trader."

"Marisol, *no debes ser abusadora.* Don't take advantage. Mrs. Trader has been very kind to you already."

"I didn't ask. She said that she didn't have anything to do but bake pies all day."

Mami raised an eyebrow. "Doesn't she have any family?"

"She does, but they don't seem to be around."

"Maybe they live far away. The way we live far away from Abuela."

I paused. It never occured to me that with most of the

family in New York, Abuela was as alone in Panama as Mrs. Trader was here.

"We should invite her over to dinner," Mami said.

"Okay."

"When you called, I was sure that you were calling from the Rosarios' to say that you were staying over there for dinner."

"Naah," I said, shaking my head. "Magda's not talking to me right now."

"What's up with you two these days?" Mami asked, concerned.

"Nothing," I said, shrugging. "I'm hungry. Let's eat."

I wanted to tell her about Marisa and Elizabeth and Magda's stealing those diamond earrings. I wanted to tell her that since I had come back from Panama, things hadn't been the same with me and my *mejor amiga*. But while Mami was cool, she was still a mom. So I didn't tell her anything.

"Will you mail these for me?" I asked, pointing to the stack of thank-you notes I'd written earlier in the day. "These are notes for my *quince* godparents."

"Of course! I'm so proud of you for getting them done so fast."

"I didn't know some of the addresses."

"I'll fill them in for you," Mami said, smoothing out my braids.

"Thank you so much for all you did, Mami. I'm so happy that I'm really going to have a *quince* of my own."

"It was Elsa's idea. But you're welcome, *niña*. You're growing into such a fine young woman. I want to honor you in front of all of our family and friends."

"*Gracias*, Mami. Speaking of what a fine young woman I am . . ."

"Yes?"

"Someone's asked me out on a date and I really would like to go."

"Who?"

"His name is Francisco and he's in my Latin American Literature class. He's a junior."

"Okay. Where do you want to go?"

"We want to go to the Museo del Barrio in the Bronx, Saturday afternoon."

"Give me his number. I'll talk to his mother and get back to you."

"But, Mami!" I squealed. "He's a junior! You can't call his mother!"

"Either I speak to his mother or you keep your butt at home."

She had that expression on her face. The one that meant she wasn't in a negotiating mood.

"Don't worry, Marisol-Mariposa," Mami said, breaking into a smile. "In all of my medical training, I've never heard of anyone actually dying of embarrassment!"

Despite my being *very sure* that I would be the first case, I laughed. Something told me that Francisco would be cool about it.

15

After Spanish class, I waited for Francisco. He looked so handsome with his close-cut haircut and wide smile. A week before, I'd never paid any attention to Francisco Noa. But then he spoke to me and let me know he liked me, and I could hardly think of anything but him.

"Lunch?" he asked.

"Sure."

"Let's go to my locker first."

I followed him down the hall and watched as he fumbled to open the locker. He reached in and pulled out an old-fashioned lunch box.

"What's this?" I asked as he handed it to me.

"Since lunch was so awful yesterday, I thought I would bring us something special."

"Why, Francisco, are you trying to impress me?"

"You bet."

We sat at the same table in the lunchroom where we had sat the day before. I glanced over at the table where Magda sat with Marisa and Elizabeth. Sammy Baldonado sat there as well. I turned my attention back to Francisco.

"What's for lunch?" I asked Francisco.

He opened the box and took out turkey sandwiches made with home-cooked turkey, sweet plantains, and Jamaican spice buns, spread with butter just the way I liked them.

"*Mundial*. Wow!" I exclaimed. "It's a feast."

"You deserve a feast," Francisco said, flirtatiously.

"Even if I'm only a freshman?"

"Especially because you're a freshman."

"Is that so?" I asked.

"Oh yeah, I've always liked younger women."

"Good, then you won't mind giving me your phone number?"

"Of course not."

"Francisco, my mother won't let me go on Saturday until she talks to your mother."

He laughed then. Not Eduardo's "heh-heh-heh" or Rubén's belly laugh, but a laugh that flowed as smoothly as a basketball layup.

"Now I'm embarrassed," I said, punching him on the shoulder.

"You give me your number," Francisco said. "Me and my mom will call your house tonight."

Then he laughed again.

That night, I was so nervous I could hardly stand it. We had One Pot leftovers, and I jumped every time the microwave bell rang. After dinner, the phone rang and I jumped for it. But it was Eduardo calling for Mami.

"I'm expecting a call," I whispered, handing Mami the cordless. "If another call comes through, click over." Sometimes when Mami is on the phone, she refuses to answer the other line.

Mami took the phone from my hand. "I pay the phone bill around here. I'll talk as long as I like."

"Mami, *please*."

"All right, all right. If your *novio* calls, I'll let you know."

I went into my room and got out a book on Frida Kahlo that I had borrowed from the library. I loved reading about her life, about how even though she was half German and born into the Mexican elite, she was an artist of the people. She dressed in pre-Columbian jewelry and Indian costumes. Frida Kahlo often painted pictures of herself in these costumes. I flipped through the book of paintings such as *The Wounded Deer* and *Self Portrait as Tehuana (Diego in My Thoughts.)* The more I read about women like Frida, the prouder I was to being a Latina. Then I came up with an idea: maybe for my *quince*, I could ask Tía China to wrap my braids with ribbons the way Frida did, in the style of the Oaxaca Indians.

Mami knocked on the door.

"*Teléfono*," she said, waving the cordless before me.

"Thanks," I mouthed silently, taking the phone from her. "Hello?"

"Hey, Marisol, it's Francisco."

"How ya' doing?"

"I'm good. My mom is ready to talk to your mother."

I went back into the kitchen.

"Mami, it's Francisco's mother."

I handed her the phone and pulled up the chair to listen to their conversation.

"Good evening," Mami said, politely. "Marisol tells me that you're from Balboa. We're from Panama City."

Once they had made that Panamanian bond, Mami and Francisco's mother talked forever. They talked about people they might know in common and how long they'd been in the United States. They talked about the best place in Brooklyn to buy mangos and codfish and the next presidential election in Panama. Mami told Francisco's mother about how I'd spent a year in Panama and what a great experience that had been for me. She told her about my *quince* and how I hadn't already chosen a *caballero*. Just when it seemed that Mami had been ready to share intimate stories about potty-training me, she hung up the phone.

"Nice talk?" I asked, anxiously. "Does this mean I can go on Saturday?"

"You can go," Mami said. "She's a charming woman. I look forward to meeting her in person."

I let out a big sigh of relief. "Thanks, Mami."

As we washed the dinner dishes, Mami pointed out that there were a few things we still hadn't figured out for the *quince*.

"Who's going to give you the first dance, since your father isn't here?"

Mami never brought up Papi. It was weird to hear her even refer to him. It was a perfectly clear night. I looked out the window. The moon hung long over the apartment buildings in the distance.

"Could you dance with me, Mami?"

Mami laughed. "We're a progressive family. But not *that* progressive."

"Who do you think it should be?"

"I know who would like to dance with you."

"Eduardo?"

"He's a nice guy, Marisol," Mami said, smiling. "I think I'm falling in love with him."

I didn't know what to say. "What does that mean? Is he going to come live here?"

"No, not yet," Mami said. "But he is going to be around more. He would love to dance the first waltz with you."

Eduardo wasn't so bad, but he wasn't my *papi*. He wasn't even as close to me as Tío Ricardo.

"I'll think about it," I told Mami.

"Fair enough," she said. "Who are going to be your *damas*?"

I silently rinsed off the plate in my hand and shrugged.

"I'm assuming that Magda will be your *dama de honor*."

"I don't know," I said, trying to keep the tears back.

Mami turned off the kitchen tap and turned to me.

"Tell me," she insisted.

"She's not sure she wants to be in my *quince*."

"You've been friends with Magda your whole life. She'll be in your *quince*."

"She's hanging out with other girls—and . . ." I started to tell Mami about the shoplifting, then stopped. All I needed was for Magda to think that not only was I a Goody Two-shoes, but that I'd ratted her out, too.

"Other friends are okay," Mami said. "Don't worry, by May, she'll be back and you two will be closer than ever."

"I doubt it," I said, turning back on the tap and rinsing the soapy cups that sat in the sink.

"If we do a half court, then you'll need six other *damas*."

"Tía China?"

"China's a little old to be in your court, Marisol-Mariposa."

"I don't know that many girls."

"Well, there's your cousin, Roxana."

"She's okay. I wish Ana could be in my court."

"It's hard to have friends that are far away, but the more friends you have all over the world, the more places you can call home."

16

I thought Saturday was never going to arrive. Usually, Mami had to resort to all kinds of torture to wake me up, but on this particular Saturday, I got up right away.

When I walked into the kitchen, Mami pretended to drop her coffee spoon in shock.

"But wait, this couldn't be my daughter, Sleeping Beauty?"

"Very funny. What's for breakfast?"

"Well, this is a very special occasion. You're up early. You have a date today."

"Can I have banana-coconut pancakes the way Abuela makes them?"

"I'm not half the cook your *abuela* is, but I'll see what I can do."

"Thanks, Mami," I said, giving her a hug.

After breakfast, I tried on every outfit in my closet. I ended up wearing my favorite red sweater and a pair of blue jeans. I was in the bathroom, putting on Mami's red lipstick, when the doorbell rang.

I ran out to buzz Francisco in when Mami grabbed me by the shoulder.

"Lose the lipstick—it's a bit much," she said.

"But Mami, please!"

"You're not fifteen yet. The red is too much. Put on some lip gloss. I'll get the door."

I went into the bathroom and took off the lipstick as she said. I put on clear lip gloss, and then just to get my way, I put on a little mascara and Mami's favorite perfume, too.

When I opened the bathroom door, Mami and Francisco were chatting in the hallway.

"You look great," he said, smiling approvingly.

"You smell good, too. That's my *favorite* perfume," Mami whispered as she helped me put on my coat.

"Thanks, Mami," I said, giving her a quick *besito* on the cheek.

"Back by seven," Mami said. "Don't forget you have to baby-sit Kiki tonight."

We walked into the first gallery and looked at a group of religious paintings and sculpture.

"Yo, they stole this from my Tía Matilde's living room," Francisco joked, standing in front of a gaudy red-and-orange painting with glitter and a holograph Jesus in the center.

"Your *tía* has good taste," I said, pretending to admire the painting.

"It runs in the family."

"I'm so glad."

We stood in front of a painting that showed the Virgin Mary wearing sexy black lingerie.

Francisco whistled. "Want to bet money that the Pope doesn't dig this?"

"I don't know," I wondered. "She sure looks hot."

"This is a weird room," Francisco said, looking around. "Let's move on."

We walked into the next room and I almost screamed. "It's a Frida," I said, running over to the painting in the center of the room.

"Who?" Francisco said, following me to the painting.

"Frida Kahlo. She was a Mexican-American painter who painted in the 1940s and 50s."

"You know a lot of stuff. . . ." Francisco said, turning to smile at me.

"For a freshman?"

The painting was called *Self-Portrait as a Tehuana (Diego In My Thoughts)*. It featured Frida in the traditional costume of the isthmus of Tehuantepec, her arms covered in a beautiful floral shawl with a wide pink band. Her face was framed by a lace mantilla with pink-and-white flowers tucked into the band above her forehead. On her forehead she had painted a portrait of Diego Rivera. It was a complicated painting, full of passion and sadness. Francisco and I stood there for a moment, admiring it. At least I thought we were admiring it, until Francisco began to poke fun.

"This lady looks like a dude," he began.

"You are sick! She's wearing a wedding dress."

"Look at her mustache!"

"It's a very faint one," I explained.

"It's still a mustache. . . ."

I put one hand on my hip and turned to him. "Now don't tell me you're Panamanian and you've never met a woman with a mustache."

"My Tía Matilde that I mentioned . . ."

"She has a mustache?"

"Yes," Francisco said. "My *mami* told her she should wax it, but my *tío* won't let her. He says it's sexy."

"I've heard that some men think so." I couldn't help laughing. Francisco was totally hilarious.

"This lady had one eyebrow. One big bushy eyebrow."

"Her name is Frida Kahlo!" I said, punching Francisco on the arm.

"She has a dude tattooed on her forehead. Weird."

"It's not a tattoo. That's her husband. And she just painted him on her forehead to show that she's always thinking about him."

"That's cool," Francisco said. "Would you do that for me?"

"What?"

"Paint me on your forehead."

I rolled my eyes. "They had a bizarre, obsessive-compulsive relationship!"

"Sounds romantic."

"He slept with her sister!"

"I won't sleep with your sister," Francisco said, winking at me.

"I don't have a sister!"

"My point, exactly."

We spent the whole afternoon at the museum, going through each gallery, making jokes and teasing each other. By the time we got out, it was almost four o'clock.

"Are you hungry?" Francisco asked.

"A little," I said.

"Let's go down to Manhattan. I know the perfect place."

We went down to the subway station; Francisco refused to let me even pay for the train ride.

"*Un caballero*. What a gentleman," I said.

"*Es un placer*. It's a pleasure," Franciso said smiling.

We stood on the subway platform, shifting from side to side to keep warm. Cold February breezes whipped across our faces.

"So is it just you and your mom?" he asked.

"Yeah," I answered.

"Where's your pops?"

I shrugged. "Not around. Somewhere in Panama."

"That sucks."

"I know. My *mami* has a new boyfriend."

"What's he like?"

"He's kind of nerdy, kind of goofy."

"That's not so bad," Francisco said, looking down the tracks. But there wasn't a train in sight. "My mom had a boyfriend for a while who was really rough. He used to hit me all the time."

"I'm sorry, Francisco."

"It's okay, he's gone now."

"Where's your father?" I asked.

"I don't know," he said.

The train hurtled into the station and the shiny doors opened before us. We found seats by the window, but turned to each other.

"We have a lot in common," Francisco said.

"You mean the fact that we don't know our dads?" I asked.

"That and our love of art."

"Tacky religious Latino art."

"And the chick with the mustache. I dig her."

"You're silly. But I dig her, too."

"Don't forget poetry. We both like poetry."

Francisco reached out for my hand. "I like you, Marisol," he whispered.

"I like you, too," I whispered back.

We got off the N train at Prince Street in a part of Manhattan that I'd never been to before.

"Where are we?" I asked.

"SoHo," Francisco answered.

Every where I looked the tiny streets were teeming with people. It seemed that everyone was young and wore black. It was like an ad for a hip clothing store.

I followed Francisco down the crowded streets until we got to a bright storefront. The words "Cafe Habana" were spray-painted across the window in bright colors, like graffiti, but on purpose.

Francisco walked into the restaurant with all the confidence of a grown-up. I tugged at my hand-me-down pea coat and felt all of my fourteen-and-a-half years. As we waited to be seated, Francisco turned around and ran his finger over the top of his lip.

I looked at our waitress, a heavy-set Brazilian woman with a mustache that made Frida's look faint. I burst out laughing.

The woman must not have noticed that we were laughing at her because she gave us a great table, right by the window, with the glowing bright-colored letters scrawled above our heads.

The woman handed us menus and we quickly ordered.

"Cuban sandwich and a hot chocolate," I said.

"Cuban sandwich and a coffee," Francisco said.

I couldn't believe that I felt closer to a guy than I did to my own *mejor amiga*. Maybe that was the true meaning of boyfriend: someone who was as much a friend as a boy you wanted to kiss.

The waitress put down our drinks, then I waited for her to be out of earshot.

"Can I ask you a question?" I said.

Francisco nodded. *"Claro."*

"Have you ever had someone close to you do something that you know was wrong?"

Francisco gave me a knowing look and sat back in his chair.

"Are you kidding, Marisol?" he asked. "My older brother used to deal drugs."

"Used to?" I asked.

"He's in jail now," Francisco said, taking a sip of his coffee and looking sadder than I'd ever seen him. "He was always trying to get me to 'run errands' for him. Don't think I wasn't tempted. The dough was so good."

Magda had said I was a Goody Two-shoes. I wondered if Francisco felt like a Goody Two-shoes around his brother. "Why didn't you do it?" I asked.

The waitress put down a bowl of hot bread and a small bowl of butter.

"What reason do you want first?" Francisco asked. "Because I didn't want to go to jail. 'Cause our neighborhood is full of guys who've been shot over that dealing mess." He paused for a second and looked embarrassed. "The main reason I didn't deal drugs because I knew what my brother was doing was breaking my *mami*'s heart."

Francisco reached for my hand and squeezed it across the table.

"Magda, *mi mejor amiga*, has been shoplifting. . . ." I began. Francisco cut me off.

"Leave it alone, " he said, sternly.

"Even if it means I don't have a best friend anymore?" I asked.

"Mejor estar solo qué mal acompanada," Francisco said, wagging a finger at me.

I looked up at him, surprised. *Better to be by yourself than to be in bad company.* It was a phrase my *abuela* always used. Hearing Francisco say it instantly made me feel at home with him.

"I'm having the best time, I don't want to leave," I looked down at my watch: six o'clock. No way I could eat and get back home to Brooklyn in an hour. "It's getting late."

"What time do you have to be at your baby-sitting job?" Francisco asked.

"Eight o'clock."

"Why don't you call your mom and ask her if it's okay if I bring you over there?"

I got up and made my way to the pay phone in the back. *"Hola?"* I heard Mami's voice down the line.

"Hi, it's me. I'm running a little late."

"That's okay. Where are you?"

"Cafe Habana in SoHo."

"Oh, SoHo. Very hip."

"Yeah, is it okay if Francisco takes me straight to the Moraleses'?"

"I guess that's okay. But make sure you get there on time.

It's important that you be responsible, okay?"

"Got it."

"Good. *Cuídate. Te amo.*"

"I love you too."

When I got back to the table, our food had arrived. "Everything's cool," I said. "I've just got to be there by eight."

"We can do that," Francisco said. Something in me shivered at the way he said "we." I kept going back and forth. Sometimes, like when we were at the museum and laughing at the paintings, I felt totally comfortable. He was a guy, but he was my friend. Then every once in a while he said something and I remembered that this was a date and he was a guy and I'd get all nervous inside.

I bit into my sandwich, the ham and cheese hot and gooey into my mouth. "This is delicious."

"I'm glad you like it."

"Hey, Francisco," I began. "What are you doing on May first?"

He looked at me, perplexed. "I don't know. What am I doing?"

"Well hopefully, you'll be my date for my *quinceañera.*"

Francisco smiled. "I'd be happy to. I've got experience, too."

"Really?"

"Yeah," he laughed. "My mother made me be my cousin's date at her *quinceañera* last year."

"That must have been fun."

"It wasn't so bad," he said. "The music was bumping. And

I should tell you now, I look good in a tux."

I ran my hand over his clean-shaven head. "I bet you do."

Francisco called for a check, we paid, and then dashed to the subway. We just caught the train before the doors closed shut.

We rode back into Brooklyn, mostly in silence. I stared up at the ads on the train and every once in a while, I discreetly snuck a glance at Francisco. Every time I looked, he caught me and either smiled or winked. He was a funny guy. I liked him, a lot.

He held my hand as we walked down the Moraleses' street. Then he asked me where they lived. I pointed to the brownstone on the corner. He looked at his watch: 7:45.

"We have fifteen minutes," Francisco said, mischievously.

I looked at my watch. "So we do. But it's cold out here. I'm not even trying to stand on the corner for fifteen minutes."

"Not even if I wanted to kiss you?"

I looked up at him and felt that nervous feeling again. "No, I guess that would be okay."

He kissed me then. I felt his lips, soft and cold against mine. Then I felt his tongue press between my lips, between my teeth, into my mouth. It was all warmth then. It was freezing outside, but the sun was shining in my mouth, I could feel the rays each time his tongue brushed against my gums, my teeth, my tongue. And just when I was wondering whether or not I was kissing him right, he pulled his tongue back, kissing me again with just his lips.

He looked at his watch. "Seven-forty-six."

"We've got fourteen minutes," I whispered.

"I thought you were cold?" he asked, grinning.

"Me? No. Not cold at all."

He kissed me then, again and again. Until it was 7:57, and he walked me to the Moraleses' door.

After Mr. and Mrs. Morales had left for their date, I made Kiki her favorite peanut-butter-and-banana sandwich and settled into watching *The Little Mermaid* for the thousandth time.

Kiki laid her head across my lap. As I ran my fingers through her hair, I played back the events of the day. I'd visited SoHo and the Museo del Barrio. I'd gotten to see a Frida Kahlo painting up close and Francisco had agreed to be my special *caballero* at my *quince*. We'd kissed, again and again. I reached for the Moraleses' phone to call Magda. Then I remembered she wasn't talking to me. It had been the perfect day. Perfect, except that I had no one to tell it to.

17

It had been two months since my best friend, Magda Rosario, had stopped talking to me. And all in all, I was handling things pretty well. Francisco and I had become an item, as regular as the rain. We ate lunch together every day. Mami still didn't let me go out on Friday nights, but Francisco and I spent most Saturdays together. I'd even made friends with a couple of the girls in my art class: Asya and Camille. We weren't as tight as Magda and I or Ana and I had been, but they were cool.

My *quince* was only a few weeks away, just a week after Magda's. A beautiful peach-colored invitation had come in the mail, inviting me to Magda's *quince*. But just as a guest.

She didn't ask me to be her *dama de honor*. She didn't ask me to be in her court at all. It was *cold*. Every day, I saw her hanging out with Marisa and Elizabeth and I wondered what we'd fought about that was so deep, we didn't even talk anymore.

One Friday night, just after I had dropped off Tyson from his daily walk, I ran into Mami on the street.

"I'm going over to visit Luisa and help her make *fritura*," Mami said. *Fritura* are all kinds of different little pies with meat and chicken inside. *Carimanoles* are made with yucca. *Tamales* and *empanadas* are made with corn. Magda's mom, Tía Luisa, sold her *fritura* all over the neighborhood. Her *fritura* was bangin'. Everybody knew that Tía Luisa made the best *fritura* in Brooklyn.

I glanced over at the Rosarios' house. I hadn't been inside for months. "I don't think so," I told Mami. "I'll just meet you at home."

"Come on, Marisol," Mami insisted. "The Rosarios are like family. You can't stay away forever. Luisa and Ricardo are very hurt."

"But Magda's the one who's got new friends. She's the one who's not talking to me!"

"That may be the case. But respect is respect. You are coming to visit her parents, not her. And I happen to know for a fact that she's not home. She's at the mall."

"Okay," I said reluctantly, following Mami up the steps to the Rosarios' home.

"*Mira quién es!*" Tía Luisa said, opening the door and giving me a big hug. "Long time no see, *niña*."

"I know, I've been busy, Tía Luisa. School and stuff."

"Come into the kitchen," she said, gesturing to me and Mami. "You know how it goes. It's still the same. Ricardo and his friends are still playing dominoes in the basement."

She bellowed down the steps. "Ricardo, Luisa and Marisol are here!"

"*Hola!*" Tío Ricardo called up the stairs.

In the kitchen, Tía Luisa was playing an old Tito Puente record. I hovered awkwardly by the door and hummed along to the words, "*Así me gustas.* I like it like that." I used to feel like the Rosarios' house was my second home. But I hadn't been to visit since Magda and I had fallen out. I kept being nervous that maybe she would walk in. I knew she wouldn't say anything too cold in front of *las madres*. But Magda was slick. She could cut you down without words.

"*Ven acá*, Marisol," Tía Luisa called me over. "Will you take this tray of *fritura* down to those loud guys downstairs?"

"No problem. They'll love this. It looks delicious," I said, lifting the tray. The *fritura* smelled so good, I could hardly wait to chow down myself.

"You got it?" Mami asked, concerned.

"I'm good."

I walked slowly through the kitchen and down the basement stairs.

"*Dichosos los ojos!*" Tío Ricardo said as I sat down the tray. "I thought you had forgotten all about us, Marisol."

"I could never forget you, Tío Ricardo," I said, giving him a hug and nodding hello at the men around the card table.

"Well, I hope that's enough *fritura*," I said, pointing to the dishes on the tray. "Because Tía Luisa says you guys aren't getting any more."

All the men at the table threw up their hands and pretended to be shocked. "*No me digas!* Is Luisa trying to starve us?!?"

Every week it was the same thing. Tía Luisa made *fritura* to sell. Then Tío Ricardo and his friends tried to eat up all of her profits. It was nice to know that even if Magda wasn't talking to me, some things were still the same.

I was sitting at the kitchen table grating corn for the empanadas when the telephone rang.

"*Bueno,*" Tía Luisa answered the phone. Then she quickly switched over to English. "Yes, I understand."

She went pale and looked almost expressionless. "I'll be right there. . . ."

"Yes. I'm on my way."

Mami and I looked at each other. What could it be? From the look on Tía Luisa's face, I was afraid that someone had died.

Mami got up and hugged Tía Luisa who was shaking so bad, she couldn't even hang up the phone. She kept missing the cradle. Mami hung it up for her.

"Luisa," Mami cooed. "What is it? Is everyone okay?"

Tía Luisa whispered into Mami's ear and reached for the car keys on the hook on the fridge.

"I'm going with Luisa," Mami said. "Keep an eye on Danilo."

"Where is he?" I asked.

"Probably upstairs watching TV in my room," Tía Luisa said, quietly. "Tell Ricardo that we'll be back soon."

I heard the front door slam and stood in the kitchen for a second, dazed. What could it be? What was going on? And what was Magda going to say when she came home to find me in her house? What if she came back with Marisa and Elizabeth? Oh, boy. I wasn't looking forward to that. I should have just come in, said hello to Tía Luisa and Tío Ricardo, and gone on home. Mami was dead wrong.

Well, I was here now and I'd been assigned baby-sitting duty, so there was no ducking out. Nothing to do but suck it up.

I walked down the basement steps and went over to Tío Ricardo. "My *mami* and Tía Luisa went out for a second. Tía Luisa said to tell you she'll be back soon."

Tío Ricardo turned to me, holding a domino in his hand. "Did they go to drop off *fritura* for someone?"

"I don't think so. The phone rang and Tía Luisa got it, then she left. She seemed upset. I'm supposed to watch Danilo. I just wanted to tell you."

He looked concerned. "Okay, Marisol, *gracias*. You know you must come over more often. You're family, *tú sabes*."

"I know, Tío Ricardo. *Gracias*."

I bounded up the stairs two at a time and found Danilo sitting on Tía Luisa's bed watching the Cartoon Network. Danilo was just three-and-a-half years old, but he was already the most handsome boy I'd ever seen. He was wearing a pair of overalls and was sitting about two inches from the TV screen. I pinched his caramel cheek and tousled his dark, curly hair.

"Hey there, Danilo."

"Marisol!" he said. "Where's my *mami?*"

"She went out. But she'll be back soon. Is it okay if I watch cartoons with you?"

He nodded yes, holding onto the remote control possessively. "Don't change the channel."

"I won't. But do you mind if we move a little farther away from the TV. Let's sit back like this," I said, scooting him back against the headboard on the bed. "Is that okay?"

"That's okay," he said, contentedly.

We'd watched three hours of cartoons when I heard the front door slam. Five minutes later, I heard Tío Ricardo's baritone yell. *"Eres loca?"* he screamed. "Are you crazy? Tell me if you're crazy, because I'll have you locked up with the crazy people!"

Something glass crashed onto the floor and then I heard Magda and Tía Luisa and Mami talking all at once.

"Papi, no! Papi, I'm sorry," Magda screamed.

"Ricardo, calm down," Mami said.

"Ricardo, don't, *por favor,*" Tía Luisa said.

I bounded down the stairs two at a time and ran to where Magda was cowering in the corner. She turned to me and began to sob in my arms.

"Do you know what the penalty for stealing used to be?!"

Tío Ricardo asked. "They would cut off your hand! I'll cut off your f— hand!"

"Papi, no!" Magda screamed, as Tío Ricardo tried to drag her to her feet. He slapped her hard, then, and Magda wailed like an animal being killed. I held her hand tight.

Tío Ricardo stormed into the kitchen with Tía Luisa following him. I looked across at Mami; her eyes told me that she was as shocked as I was. Magda cried, continuously and softly.

A few minutes later, Tío Ricardo returned with a large butcher's knife.

"My daughter is a thief!" Tío Ricardo screamed. "If I cut off her hand, she'll never steal again."

Magda looked up from the floor and I saw something that I'd never seen in her eyes before: fear.

Mami walked up to Tío Ricardo and slowly put a hand on his.

"Ricardo, *por favor*," she said. "Give me the knife. You know you don't want to do this. This is how people get hurt."

"I want to hurt her!" he screamed. "I want to hurt her! Because she's hurt me! Stealing! Bringing shame into my home! How could she?"

Tío Ricardo started crying then. At first I thought he was laughing, the way his body shook and the sobs tumbled out of his mouth. But then I saw that he was crying, for real. He put the knife down, then dropped to the floor. Mami picked up the knife and took it back into the kitchen. Then she sat down on the floor with Magda, Tío Ricardo, and Tía Luisa.

Since it seemed to be the thing to do, I plopped down on the floor too.

Tía Luisa slid next to Tío Ricardo and grabbed hold of his hand. "I came to this country, illegally," Tío Ricardo said, quietly. "I lived in a one-room apartment with four other men until I could bring your mother to this country. I worked in a factory for less than minimum wage. I pumped gas at night. I cleaned *toilets*. I never once stole even a piece of bread even when I didn't have a piece of bread!"

"*Yo sé*, Papi. I know," Magda said, in a voice that made it clear she'd heard his immigrant-made-good story before.

"You know!" Tío Ricardo barked out. He jumped up and started to shake Magda so hard, I thought the teeth were about to fall out of her mouth.

"Ricardo, *cálmate!*" Tía Luisa said, pulling him off of Magda.

"You don't know!" he continued. "You don't know! But you will know. I am calling off your *quince*. Why should I pay to celebrate a thief?"

All of the women in the room sat there stunned. Then Magda went into full beg mode.

"Please, Papi. Not my *quince*."

"You said you know. I want you to know what true sacrifice is."

Tía Luisa put a hand on Tío Ricardo's shoulder. "I agree that she must be punished, Ricardo. But the *quince* isn't the way. We've bought a dress. We put a deposit down on the banquet hall, the caterers, the florists. It's only two weeks away, we will lose thousands of dollars."

"I don't care," Tío Ricardo said, standing up. "I don't care about the money. A *quinceañera* is a celebration to honor your daughter. I will *not* honor this daughter!"

He turned around and walked out of the room.

"Don't let him do this, Mami," Magda sobbed. "He can't cancel my *quince*."

"We'll see," Tía Luisa said, cradling Magda against her chest. "He's mad at you. I'm mad at you, too."

Mami stood and I rose as well.

"Te hablo mañana," Mami said, kissing Tía Luisa on the cheek. "I'll call you."

I wanted to say something to Magda, but I wasn't sure what. Then she spoke to me. "'Bye, Marisol."

Mami and I walked down the street in silence. The street lamps bobbed like white pumpkins in the dark.

"How did he know?" I asked.

"Luisa got a call from the department store security. They caught Magda and her friends, Marisa and Elizabeth, stealing. Turns out that they've been keeping track of them for months now. They had stolen so many valuable things, it was a felony. They were going to send them to jail."

I stopped short. "A felony?"

Mami turned to me. "How long have you known that Magda's been shoplifting?"

I continued walking.

"Is that why you and Magda stopped spending time together?"

I nodded.

"When were you going to tell me?" Mami asked as we rode up the elevator to our apartment.

"I didn't know how."

Mami opened the front door to our apartment then closed it behind her.

"Did you ever steal with her, Marisol? Tell me the truth."

"No, never!" How could Mami ask me such a thing?

"You're not just saying that because you're afraid I might cancel your *quince* too?"

"I'm saying it because it's the truth! How could you doubt me, Mami? You raised me better than that."

Mami looked into my eyes and then spoke. "I'm sure that's what Luisa and Ricardo are thinking right now. That they raised their daughter better than that. I need you to come to me, Marisol. There's nobody in this house but you and me. We've got to trust each other. No matter how bad it is, come to me."

I nodded. "Okay, Mami. I'm going to go to bed if that's okay."

"Okay, Marisol-Mariposa. *Te amo*."

"I love you too, Mami."

Then we hugged each other for a long time and did not let go.

18

The next morning, Mami didn't wake me the way she usually did. In fact, she let me sleep all afternoon. When I finally got up, it was two o'clock. I walked into the dining room, where Mami was sewing *capias* for my *quinceañera*. I picked up a ribbon and smiled at the inscription. It said "Marisol's *Quinceañera*, May 1st," and there was a picture of a red butterfly after the birth date.

"Good morning, Sleeping Beauty," Mami said. I went over and gave her a kiss.

"When did you get these?" I asked, holding up a ribbon. "They're cool."

"Alicia dropped them off this morning. How'd you sleep?"

"Not so good. I kept thinking about Magda. Last night was rough."

Mami shook her head. "I still can't believe it."

I sat down at the dining room table and played with a *capia*. "Do you think Tío Ricardo will really call off Magda's *quince*?"

Mami gave me a serious look. "Do I think he'll do it? It's already done. I spoke to Luisa and early this morning, Ricardo canceled the hall, the flowers. He even drove to the mall and returned Magda's dress. It's costing them a small fortune to call off the *quince* at such a late date. But he's intent on teaching Magda a lesson."

I shivered. I knew Magda. She'd been dreaming about her *quince*, as I had, all of her life. She'd never doubted that she was going to have one. Her sister Evelyn had had a *huge quince*.

"She must be devastated," I said.

"She got into serious trouble, Marisol. Let's not forget."

"I know, Mami. But it just seems so extreme."

"Not compared to jail, it's not."

Jail. The very thought creeped me out.

"You better shower," Mami said. "Eduardo is on his way over."

I had agreed, maybe against my better judgment, to dance my first waltz with Eduardo. Mostly because I knew it would make Mami happy. But also, I admit, because he was starting to grow on me. In exchange, Eduardo had promised to call me Marisol. Not Marisolita or Mari-boom or any of the other stupid names that he had come up with. Now, with only two weeks to go before my *quince*, he was coming over to practice dancing with me. Mrs. Trader was going to sing the first song. I'd picked Dinah Washington's "I Remember You." We'd practiced dancing to the song so many times that I knew all the words by heart.

"Okay, I'll be right out," I said, ducking into the bathroom. "I'm hungry. Can we order a pizza?"

"No, I've got *fritura* left over from last night. Go take a shower and I'll warm it up."

I came out of the shower, dressed in my favorite pair of navy sweat pants and an orange rugby. My braids hung in a ponytail behind me. I smelled the *fritura* before I saw them, golden and delicious on a platter on the table. I reached for a napkin and picked up an *empanada*.

"Hmmm, beef *empanada*, my favorite." I said, biting in.

"Don't forget to save some for Eduardo," Mami said, looking over a pile of my *quince* ribbons she was sewing onto the *capias*.

"Eduardo can get his own *fritura*," I said, pulling the platter toward me. "We went through a lot of drama last night to get these *empanadas* and *tamales*."

"Marisol!" Mami said. "Show some manners, *por favor*."

"Kidding. I'm just kidding."

The doorbell rang and I jumped up to answer it. "Who is it?" I called into the intercom.

"Soy yo, Eduardo."

I buzzed him in. I walked over to the stereo and turned on the tape of Dinah Washington songs that Mrs. Trader had made for me.

Mami opened the front door for Eduardo. Immediately, he dove into the plate of *fritura*.

"Hey, save some for me!" I called out from the living room, where I was moving the coffee table to make room for our dance practice.

"Marisol!" Mami reprimanded.

"Just save me one beef *empanada*," I said. Eduardo wasn't a huge guy, but as Abuela would say, he ate like a soul inspired.

"Hola, Marisol!" Eduardo called out and I yelled hello back. From the living room I could hear Mami fluttering back and forth in English and Spanish, telling Eduardo all about the previous evening's drama at the Rosarios'. Every once in a while he chimed in with a *"No me digas"* or "What happened next?"

Eventually they moved into the living room and we began to practice our waltz.

"Tell me again, why the first dance isn't going to be a Latin classic?" Eduardo said, holding my arms in a stiff, formal pose.

"Because it's called the first waltz, not the first booty shake," Mami reminded him.

"But I'm a better salsa dancer than a waltzer," Eduardo complained.

"Ain't that the truth," Mami said to no one in particular.

It was just the sort of thing that I would get in trouble for saying. But it was true. Funny thing about Eduardo, he was great at dancing to fast tunes: salsa, cumbia, merengue. He could do them all. But when you slowed the music down, he became the world's biggest klutz. There was no explaining it. But really, I didn't mind. I figured the worse he danced, the better it made me look.

The doorbell rang again and I raised an eyebrow at Mami. I wasn't expecting company. Mami got up and went to the intercom. A few seconds later, Tía China came through the front door. The last time I'd seen her, she had had long, dark hair. Now she was sporting a head full of spirally red curls.

Eduardo and I stopped dancing to kiss our hellos, but Tía China took a seat next to Mami and insisted we keep going.

"Don't let me interrupt you," she said out loud. Then to Mami, she whispered, "Looks like you need all the practice you can get."

Eduardo and I both turned around and said, "We heard that."

Tía China threw her head back and giggled, her head full of curls bouncing with her. "It was meant for you to hear!"

After about an hour, we'd both had enough of the waltz, and Mami had put on a tape of classic salsa tunes. She danced with Eduardo and Tía China danced with me. We were just working up a good sweat when the doorbell rang again. Mami went to the intercom and buzzed the door open. A few minutes later, when I opened the door to our apartment, I saw that it was Francisco.

"*Buenos días,*" he called out to all the grown-ups, and then he turned to me and said more casually, "Hey, Marisol, what's up?"

I was surprised. We hadn't made a date, and I'd talked to him right before I went into the shower.

"What are you doing here?" I asked, fidgeting with my rugby shirt, which was starting to seem really old and ratty to me. If I had known Francisco was coming, I would have dressed a little more carefully.

"You're not glad to see me?" he asked, innocently.

"Of course, I am!" I said, kissing him on the cheek. "But you never just drop by."

"I was bored at home, so I thought I would surprise you."

"That's cool," I said. "Come into the living room."

I introduced Francisco to Tía China, whom he'd never met before, and he chatted for a few minutes with Mami and Eduardo. We all danced for a while to a tape of new Latin music that Tía China had gotten from a DJ friend of hers, then the bell rang again. Now I was all-out suspicious. There was definitely something going on, but what? My *quince* was a two full weeks away and I couldn't think of a bigger surprise than the night when I met all my *padrinos* and found out that despite our lack of money, I was going to have a *quince* after all.

When I opened the door, it was Tía Alicia with my little cousin, Jason.

"We came to make *capias*," Tía Alicia explained.

"Mami said you had candy at your house," Jason added.

I kissed them both.

"*Capias* are there," I pointed to the table. "And Jason, if you come with me, I'll show you my extra-secret, only-for-superheroes stash of candy."

He squealed with delight as I led him into the kitchen.

When Mami came into the kitchen to get drinks for Tía Alicia and Eduardo, I cornered her.

"What's going on?" I asked.

"What do you mean?" she said innocently, too innocently for a *mami*. When there's really nothing to tell, she's far more flip, and says things like, "I'm the mother, you're the child. I ask the questions around here."

"Why do we have all these uninvited guests?"

Mami winked at me. "Who said they're uninvited?"

Back in the living room, I sidled up to Francisco and asked him, "Did my *mami* invite you over?"

"I was just in the neighborhood. . . ." he insisted, but the smile on his face said differently.

Around six o'clock, the phone rang. Mami called out, "Marisol, it's for you. Why don't you take it in my bedroom?"

I picked up the phone next to Mami's bed and said, "Hello?"

"Marisol, it's me, Magda."

It had been so long since she had called me on the phone, I was shocked.

"How are you, Magda?"

She sniffled and I could tell she'd been crying nonstop.

"Not good, Marisol. Not good. My *papi* canceled my

quince. Everything: the hall, the caterers, the photographer. He even took my dress back to the store."

"I'm really sorry, Magda."

"I screwed up so bad. I never made such a big mistake in my life. And now for one mistake, I've ruined my whole entire *quince*." She started to cry again and I could barely hear her words through the sobs. I felt terrible. We were practically having a party at my house and at Magda's, there were only tears. Even Tío Ricardo had cried!

"I'm so sorry, Magda. Maybe he'll change his mind."

"He's not changing his mind!" she sobbed. "He took all of my *capias* and threw them into the Dumpster on the street. Those cost hundreds of dollars. He's not going to change his mind."

"Wow," I said sucking in my breath, and wondering what would have happened if I knew my father and had gotten into the kind of trouble that Magda had. That's the thing about *papis*. They were strict. *Mamis* would cut you a lot more slack.

"I didn't think it was a big deal," Magda continued. "Taking a lipstick here and a pair of earrings there. I know you weren't into it, but Marisol, it was *so* much fun. Every time I thought we'd get caught and we didn't, it made it that much more exciting. The more I didn't get caught, the more I felt like I'd never be caught."

"What were you stealing last night?"

"Diamond tennis bracelet to go with my earrings. I thought I was so slick. I'd slipped it into my shirt sleeve and

I was halfway to the bus stop when the store security guard came after us. Then Marisa said, 'Run,' so we all started to run, which was stupid. We could have gotten shot."

I thought of the rent-a-cops that worked security at the mall. I don't think most of them even carried a gun. But I didn't say anything.

"Do you think your mother would let you be in my *quince?*" I asked. "I'd still like you to be my *dama de honor.*"

"Oh," Magda said tentatively. "I don't know if I could bear to be in another *quince* with mine canceled. But if my *papi* says it's okay, maybe I could be in yours."

For a few seconds, there was just silence on the phone. I didn't know what to say. So much had happened. For months, I'd been angry with Magda for not being a good friend to me. But now, I just felt sorry for her. No *quince?* That was a punishment worse than death.

Finally, Magda spoke. "I can't believe you would even have me after the way I treated you."

"You *did* treat me pretty awfully," I said.

"I'm so sorry. The last six months have been such a roller-coaster ride," Magda said. "Sometimes, I felt so cool, so grown. Other times, I just felt like I was playing a role. I can't really explain it. But *te amo*, Marisol."

"I love you too, Magda." And the funny thing was, I really meant it.

At seven o'clock, we still had a full house. Mami was cooking up a storm in the kitchen. Eduardo and Tío Diego were in the living room listening to music and talking. Jason was taking a nap in Mami's bedroom. Tía China and Tía Alicia were making *capias*. When Francisco came over, Mami only let him sit in my room if the door was open. So that's where we were, sitting in front of the open door to my room, allegedly looking at art books, but really stealing kisses.

I went into the kitchen and told Mami that I'd better get ready to go to the Moraleses'.

"Didn't I tell you?" she asked. "They called. They don't need you to baby-sit Kiki tonight."

"But I didn't hear the phone ring!"

Mami put her hand on her hip. "You're too young to be going deaf. Believe me, it rang."

There was definitely something strange going on, but clearly no one was going to tell me. I decided to just go with the flow.

"Can Francisco stay for dinner?" I asked.

"*Claro*," Mami said. "He's always welcome. Make sure he calls his mother."

"Mami! He's sixteen. He doesn't call home every five minutes to tell his mother where he is."

"When he's at my house, he does."

I walked back to my room and told Francisco, "There's good news and bad news."

"Always the good news first," he said.

"The good news is that I don't have to baby-sit and if you're not busy, we'd love for you to stay for dinner."

"*Excelente*," he said. "What's the bad news?"

"My *mami* insists on treating you like a baby. She says you have to call your mom and tell her where you're at."

"I think I can handle that," Francisco said. "I'll call her from the kitchen."

I sat at the dining room table with my *tías*. Even though he was spitting distance away, they began to talk about him as if he wasn't even there.

"I like your *novio*," Tía China began.

"He seems like a nice boy."

"Nice? He's *cute*."

"He's well-mannered."

"A good-looking, well-mannered Panamanian boy," Tía China laughed. "Marisol, you definitely picked the boy most likely to impress your family."

I laughed along with her, but in my heart, I knew that I hadn't so much picked Francisco as he had picked me. If he hadn't talked to me after Spanish class, he would have been just another junior who intimidated the heck out of me.

As Francisco joined us at the table, the doorbell rang again. Tía China jumped up and buzzed the door open.

"You didn't even ask who it was?" I said, dumbfounded. "Mami would kill me if I ever buzzed the door open like that."

"But I know who it is," Tía China said, grinning.

"How?" I insisted.

She tossed her curls and pointed one perfectly manicured fingernail toward her temple. "I'm psychic."

The doorbell to our apartment rang and I opened it.

First, my cousins Roxana and Manuel walked in. Then my Tía Julia walked in. I was about to close the door before her, when I saw a thin, caramel-colored hand that I would know even if I were blind *and* asleep. I threw the door open and screamed.

"Abuela!" I pulled her tiny frame into the house and held her so tight, I almost squeezed the life out of her. Then I promptly burst into tears.

"I come all the way from Panama and she cries," Abuela said, jerking a thumb in my direction.

"I'm—crying—because—I'm happy," I flubbed the words, trying to talk with a snotty nose and wet eyes. "No one told me."

"Of course, no one told you. That's what makes it a surprise," Tía China said.

"Well, my youngest granddaughter is having a big fancy *quinceañera* at some place called the Brooklyn Lodge, I had to come," Abuela said. "If it was winter, I wouldn't have come. I can't stand New York in the winter. But the spring I could manage. I like to see all the flowers in bloom. Most beautiful of all, my granddaughter is in bloom."

I held onto Abuela's hand and for the rest of the night, I didn't let it go unless it was absolutely necessary. We stayed up eating and dancing and talking until it was almost daylight. Tío Diego and Tía Alicia drove Francisco home. Tía Julia gave Tía China a ride. Eduardo left with a plastic container of leftovers minutes before daybreak. I gave Abuela my bed, then snuggled up in a sleeping bag on the floor beside her.

"I can't believe you're here, Abuela," I whispered. "It's like a dream."

"Nonsense," Abuela said, running her fingers through my braids. "In two weeks time, you will be honored as a young woman in the community. My *quinceañera* princess. You're the dream come true."

19

The night before my *quinceañera*, I don't think I slept at all. Mami had tried to get me to go to bed early, but there was just no way. I talked on the phone to Francisco. I watched music videos. I talked on the phone to Magda, then I sketched in my notebook. I danced around the apartment, practicing my merengue.

"You'll wake up looking tired with dark circles underneath your eyes!" Mami had warned.

"That's what makeup is for!" I saucily replied. "Mami, asking me to go to sleep now is like sending little Jason to bed early on Christmas Eve!"

"Do you hear this?" Mami had said, appealing to Abuela to take her side.

Abuela sat on the reclining chair and shook her head. "My name's Bennett and I'm not in it."

I laughed and gave Abuela a *besito* on the cheek.

"Help me out, here," Mami implored. "She needs her beauty sleep."

"The name's Bennett and I'm not in it," Abuela repeated, winking at me.

Mami just rolled her eyes, then stomped into the kitchen, where she was baking a fruitcake. She did an about-face back into the living room and glared at Abuela. "Your name's Velásquez, not Bennett."

Eventually, around midnight, I went to bed, but I didn't close my eyes. I jumped up and lifted the plastic off of my dress. I kept wanting to try it on and take it off and try it on again. But Mami was so afraid I might get stains on it, she said I had better not.

I turned on the light by my bed and flipped slowly through my *quince* dream book. Almost all that I dreamed of was about to come true. I had everything, except for my *papi*. I'd gone all the way to Panama and I hadn't found him. I had left letters and said prayers on my rosary and still he hadn't showed up. I had celebrated my fifteenth birthday and would be presented as a young woman to all of our family and friends and he was nowhere to be found.

I pulled the one photo I had of him out of my night-table drawer. He was standing with Mami, in front of a shiny new car. Mami was only seventeen, just two years older than I am now. Papi was eighteen. Mami and I grow older, but he stays the same. In my head, he is always young and handsome, about to drive away in a shiny new car. And on the night of my *quinceañera*, I would dance my first waltz with a man who was not my father. "I'm sorry, Papi," I whispered to the photo. "I'm not trying to replace you. It's just that you're not here and Eduardo is. I know you understand."

I put the photo away and drifted off to sleep.

When my eyes opened at eight the next morning, everyone was awake but me.

"Good, you're up!" Tía China said, poking her head into my bedroom door. "I've been wanting to turn up my music, but your Mami wouldn't let me."

"Arrrgh," I mumbled, turning in my bed and pulling the covers over my head once more.

Mami came in and raised the blinds, then in one swift move, she yanked the blanket off of me. "Come on, *quince* girl. We've got a lot to do."

She held out a bathrobe for me to put on. "Take a shower and don't take forever. Not if you want China to do that crazy hairstyle."

"I do, I do."

I jumped in the shower and washed everything twice. I stepped into the bathroom full of steam and wiped the mirror with my hand. I looked at myself in the mirror and carefully studied every nook and cranny on my face. There *were* dark circles underneath my eyes, but luckily no pimples. Not yet. Tía China had done my braids the week before, so they were fresh and smooth. I put on the bathrobe and went into the kitchen.

"*Feliz cumpleaños,*" Tía Julia said, giving me a kiss as she deftly fried *ajolas*, Panamanian biscuits, and turkey bacon in the cast-iron skillet on the stove. "Breakfast will be ready soon."

"*Felicidades,*" greeted Abuela, as she stirred pancake batter at the counter. "I'm making banana-and-coconut pancakes. Your favorite."

"Happy Birthday!" Mami joined in, wrapping me in a bear hug. "Go start with your hair in the living room and I'll bring breakfast out. I just spoke to Luisa. Magda's on her way."

Tía China had turned up the music. A suave mariachi sang, "*Bandelero, bandelero, por tú soy . . .*" and I smiled at the song of the man who loses his beloved because his best friend gave her more attention. Maybe it was because I had just turned fifteen. Maybe it was because of Francisco, but grown-up love songs made more sense to me than they used to.

Tía China sat at an open window with a book and a cup of coffee. "I've been looking at pictures of your artist friend, Frida Kahlo."

"Do you think you can do the hairstyle?"

"*I* can do any hairstyle," Tía China boasted.

Tía Julia came into the living room with two plates of food. She handed them to Tía China and me, then picked up the book on Frida Kahlo that I'd brought home from the library.

"Tell me again, why you want your hair in this crazy style," Tía Julia asked.

"Frida Kahlo always dressed in native Mexican costumes," I explained.

"But you're not Mexican!" Tía Julia exclaimed. She was the most conservative of all my *tías*. Mami says it's because she's the oldest.

I bit into a hot *ajola* and sloppily wiped the butter running down my cheek. I could eat butter and *ajolas* fresh from the pan all day long.

"I know I'm not Mexican," I said, covering my mouth with my hand as I finished chewing my food. "But I want to show pride in my Latina heritage."

"What does 'Latina' mean?" Tía Julia asked. She took off her apron; underneath she wore a perfectly ironed light-gray sleeveless dress. A matching jacket hung on a hook, by the door. "If you're so patriotic, wear *timbales* and a *pollera* to your *quince*, the way a true Panamanian girl would."

"But Frida Kahlo didn't wear a *pollera*!" I exclaimed.

"Aha," Tía Julia said. "The point isn't to show pride as a Latina, but to copy her."

Mami came in with a glass pitcher of freshly squeezed orange juice.

"Marisol wants to be an artist," she told Tía Julia. "I think the hairstyle is very creative."

"I don't like these paintings," Tía Julia sniffed. "They're very depressing."

"Enough talk already!" Tía China said. "Marisol, *ven acá*.

Let's get started already."

I sat on the floor in front of Tía China and unwrapped the bags of ribbon we had bought several weeks before. The ribbon matched my *quince* dress perfectly. I ran my finger along each cranberry-red seam.

As Tía Julia and Mami debated the pros and cons of my becoming an artist, Tía China created a masterpiece on top of my head. She deftly sculpted my braids into smooth shiny rolls that crisscrossed around the crown of my head. Then she snaked the ribbon through each roll until you could not tell where my hair began and the ribbon began. In less than thirty minutes she was done.

Mami stood up from her windowsill perch and gave me a hug. "*Mi niña*, the most creative *quince* of them all."

"It's beautiful," Abuela said. "Tell me again where this hairstyle is from?"

"It's a style worn by women from Oaxaca," I explained.

"We're not from Oaxaca," Tía Julia muttered. She examined my head from the back, the front, and then proclaimed. "It's lovely, anyway."

I dashed to the bathroom to look in the mirror. I was blown away. I'd never worn my hair all piled on top of my head like this before. I loved the way the red ribbon played off of my golden-brown braids. I looked older than I had looked last week, when I was just fourteen. I looked older than fifteen even. I looked older and I looked glamorous. Like a real Brooklyn *campesina*: part homegirl, part traditional girl.

I ran back into the living room and buried Tía China with

besitos. "I love it! I love it! I love it!"

"You're welcome, *niña*," she said. "Anything for you."

The doorbell rang and Mami buzzed the intercom. "It's Magda. I'm going to go get dressed. It's already ten o'clock and we're due at the church at twelve."

I opened the door for Magda. Before she'd even said hello, she was touching my hair. "Mayaguez, this is *so* cool. Not you setting styles!"

Magda greeted all the *tías* and my *abuela,* then we went into the bedroom to get dressed. She opened the garment bag she had been carrying and laid her dress across my bed. I had chosen strapless silver dresses for my *damas.* Magda would almost prefer to have bamboo shoots stuck underneath each fingernail than to wear silver, but she admitted that the dresses were pretty. I had also decided not to have a full court or even half a court. I would have just two *damas*: Magda and my cousin Roxana.

Abuela knocked on the bedroom door. "Be very careful putting on those dresses, *niñas.*" We promised we would.

For the occasion, Mami had bought me new, fancy underwear from the grown-up section of the store where she shopped. I slipped them on and then sat back on the bed, carefully pulling on my stockings so I didn't make a run. Magda sat across from me, doing the same thing.

"How are things?" I asked.

She shrugged. "Still bad. My *papi* barely speaks to me and when he does, it's with this incredibly sad look. As if I'd murdered someone."

"I still can't believe he canceled your *quince*."

Magda cringed. "I know. I cried all last Saturday night. I couldn't believe I was home watching TV instead of dancing with Sammy in the Parker Ballroom, having the best night of my life."

"I'm sorry."

"This is going to sound stupid, but I cried last night too. I kept wondering how I would feel being a *dama* in your *quince*, when I didn't even have my own."

"I know what you mean," I said, looking into the eyes of the girl who had been my best friend for as long as I could remember. The same girl who had been my worst enemy for a short time that I could never forget.

"I guess this is what you felt like when you didn't know if you were going to be able to afford a *quince*."

I nodded.

"I'm sorry, Marisol. I'm sorry about all the mean things Marisa said." Magda turned toward the window and looked away from me. "Serves me right, doesn't it? Having my *quince* canceled when I was so mean."

I went over to her and saw she was crying. Not a sob or a muffled cry, just crystal tears pouring steadily down her cheeks.

"Magda, your *quince* wasn't canceled because you were mean to me. Though you were. It was canceled because you were arrested for shoplifting. You could have gone to *jail*. That had nothing to do with me."

"I know," Magda said, throwing her arms around me. "I know."

Tía China came into the room and clapped her hands. "*Apúrate!* We've got to hurry now."

Magda and I just stood there in our slips, crying like babies.

"No tears!" Tía China said. "Not on the dresses!" She went to the bathroom, then came back with a roll of toilet paper. Magda and I started to crack up.

"What?" Tía China said. "There's no Kleenex in this house. Wipe your eyes and put on your dresses. We've still got your makeup to do."

First, I helped Magda slip her dress over her head. Then she helped me. When we walked out of my bedroom, holding hands, everyone in the dining room applauded. Mami opened the closet door so we could see ourselves in the full-length mirror. Thin satin straps fell delicately over each of my shoulders; the straight red sheath made me look even taller than I am, and far more glamorous than I thought I could ever be. Beside me, Magda's bare shoulders shimmered above a river of silver satin. We turned to hug each other and just when I thought I would burst into tears again, I felt a flash go off in my eyes.

"Picture time!" Tía China cried out.

"Not without our makeup!" Magda insisted.

And everyone—Abuela, Tía Julia, Mami, me—laughed and laughed.

What with all the picture-taking and talking, getting our makeup done and our nails done, we barely made it to the church on time. Mami had requested a special *misa* in honor of my *quinceañera*. As we entered the church, we were handed programs that not only had my name on it, but my picture too. It was then that I started to feel nervous; every muscle in my hands was shaking. Mami put her arm around me and guided me down the center aisle.

There were some strangers in the church—it was still a regular mass, it's just that at the end we would have the *quince* ceremony. But the closer we got to the front, the more faces I recognized. Mrs. Trader was there, sitting with Mami's work friend, Mrs. Dove. Magda's whole family was there: Tía Luisa, Tío Ricardo, Danilo, her brother Rogelio. Magda waved at me, then went to sit with them. The Moraleses were there. So were Mami's friends: Leticia and Mauricio Vega. Tío Diego was there with my cousin Jason. My cousins Roxana and Manuel were there. Roxana winked at me and pointed to her silver *dama* dress. When we got to the front row, there were two men seated. Eduardo and Francisco, both dressed in formal charcoal-gray tuxedos. I kissed them both on the cheek, then Mami and I sat with them. I could not get over the look on Francisco's face. He looked like a guy who'd found a winning lottery ticket in a Cracker Jack box. I couldn't help but wish that he'd been at the house earlier this morning. I would not have needed a single mirror to tell me how beautiful I looked. It was all in his eyes.

Padre Delano went through the mass, but it was hard for me to pay attention. He went through the order of confession and the sharing of the peace. He read from the Old Testament and the New Testament, and then he turned to me.

"Today, I am honored to present one of our faithful congregation as a *quinceañera* today," he said.

He called me up to the altar. As tradition required, Tía Julia handed me the bouquet of red roses we had brought along.

I placed each rose, fifteen in all, at the feet of the Virgin Mary. Then I read the prayer of thanksgiving.

Padre Delano asked the congregation to pray for me as I entered womanhood, then he called for the presentation of the traditional gifts.

Mami came up to the lectern and spoke into the microphone. "This is the *quinceañera* rosary and Bible. Carry them with you and remember God's word."

She placed the new Bible and rosary in my hand. She hugged me and turned to move away. But I didn't want her to go. As excited as I was, I felt scared all alone at the altar with Padre Delano. Maybe I wasn't ready to walk the path of womanhood, after all. *"No te preocupes, farolito,"* Mami said, reading either my mind or the way my body trembled. "You look beautiful. You'll be just fine."

Eduardo came up to the lectern and said, "This is the crown. Remember as you move through your teenage years, that no matter what challenges face you, you are worthy. You are a queen in the eyes of God."

He placed the crown on my head, a thin silver tiara with sparkling rhinestones. I kissed him on the cheek and he sat down.

Tía Alicia went to the lectern and presented a medal depicting San Antonio de Padua. "This is the medal of faith," she said. Then she tied the medal around my neck.

Abuela stood then and the smile she gave me was so wide that I thought I could lose myself in her joy. "I am Señora Velásquez. I am the grandmother. These earrings are to remind you to listen to God's word. This bracelet represents the never ending circle not only of God's love, but my love as well."

She came to the altar, petite but strong, and handed me beautiful gold earrings that I recognized as handmade in Panama. I placed them in my ears. Then she fastened the bracelet on my wrist. "I could not be prouder," she whispered as she held me close. "*Gracias*, Abuela." I whispered back. "I love you."

Padre Delano rose and called Mami to the altar once more. "Now is the time for the changing of the shoes."

Mami opened the plastic bag that she had carried in and took out a pair of cranberry-red high heels that she'd had dyed to match my dress.

She approached the altar and Padre Delano blessed the shoes.

She took off the flats that I was wearing, then slipped a satin pump on each foot. If I had not felt like Cinderella before, I felt like her then. Mami winked at me, then took the flats away.

Padre Delano took my hand and when I stood, I was literally, spiritually, emotionally, taller than I had been before. Everywhere I looked in the church, there was a smiling face and I felt bathed in love.

If this was a movie, I thought, as the organ began to play the recessional hymn, my *papi* would be out there, in a back row. He would have slipped in to see the ceremony and now that it was done, he would slip out again.

And although it wasn't a movie, I decided to pretend that was what had happened. Because I wanted him here, even if only as part of my fantasy.

"Your childhood days are done," Padre Delano said. "You have put away childish things. You walk the path of womanhood now. But you do not walk alone. You walk with God and with this congregation that offers you its helping hand."

I walked down the altar steps as people began to file out of the church. There were many *besos* and *abrazos* to give, hugs and kisses all around. But when it was all said and done, I took Francisco's hand. In *quinceañera* tradition, it is the *caballero*, the gentleman who walks the *quinceañera* out of the church.

Hours later, after a professional photographer had spent hours snapping photos of all of us at the Botanical Garden and Eduardo had finished filming the whole thing with his video camera, we went to the reception. We arrived by limousine, just as Mrs. Dove had promised. The Brooklyn Lodge was decorated in red and silver balloons, tablecloths, and streamers. Silver stars, like the kind your teacher gives you in second grade when you get an A on a book report, were strewn by the thousands across the dance floor.

I went over to Magda, who was seated at a table with Sammy Baldonado. *"Feliz Cumpleaños,"* Sammy said, giving me a kiss on my cheek.

"Gracias," I answered. "Magda, come to the bathroom with me?"

She followed me into the bathroom. I could hear the growing chatter of people coming in and taking their seats.

"You're shiny," Magda said, taking a compact out of her purse.

She dabbed powder on my forehead, then stepped back and looked me up and down.

"You look beautiful," she said, smiling. *"Bellísima."*

"I'm sorry your *quince* was canceled," I said, straightening the tiny gold cross around her neck.

"I'm not going to lie," she said, turning away from me and staring at her own reflection in the mirror. "When I saw you stepping out of that limousine at the church, I just wished it was me."

I put my arms around Magda and held her tight. I'd spent so much of this year envying Magda, wishing that I was as confident as she was and that I had the money that her family did. All that time, I never thought I'd see the day when Magda might be jealous of me.

"Close your eyes and look up," Magda said, opening a wand of mascara.

As she darkened my lashes with mascara, she began to sing one of our favorite songs, Fiona Apple's "Criminal."

" 'I've been a bad, bad girl,' " Magda began in her sultry deep voice.

" 'And it's a sad, sad world,' " I joined in. " 'When a girl will break a boy just because she can.' "

By the time Tía China entered the bathroom, we'd already stumbled through three verses of the song: skipping the parts we didn't know, making up the words we couldn't remember.

"The show's out there, ladies," Tía China said, laughing and pointing to the ballroom.

"We know," Magda said, hooking her arm into mine. "We were just warming up."

As we walked back into the ballroom, I thought of what a perfect expression that was. My friendship with Magda still had a lot of kinks to work out. But we were getting there, after freezing each other out for so long, we were finally beginning to warm up to the idea of being *mejores amigas* once again.

When everyone had taken their seats, Mrs. Trader made her way onto the stage. A young man I recognized from the photos in her house played piano. She began the first verse of "I Remember You," and Eduardo stood and asked me to dance. I took his hand, the way we had practiced so many times before and he walked me to the center of the dance floor. And just as we began to glide across the floor, the strangest thing happened.

Live butterflies began to swirl around us. They were all colors: red, blue, orange, and green. I stopped dancing and looked around in wonder as the whole room began to clap. I tried to figure out where the butterflies had come from and then I noticed two women who were releasing them from glass boxes at each of the side doors.

"Never been upstaged by a butterfly before," Mrs. Trader purred into the microphone. "Let's start this number again."

Eduardo took my hand again and we danced the first waltz as gracefully and gloriously as I had imagined it. And every time I thought of my *papi*, every time I thought I might cry, I would catch a glimpse of a butterfly and smile instead.

"Happy birthday, Marisol-Mariposa," he said, calling me the name that only Mami used.

"*Gracias*, Eduardo," I answered as he spun me around and around.

And that is how I celebrated my fifteenth birthday. I spent the whole night dancing on a blanket of silver stars. In a circle of friends and family. Heralded by butterflies. Transformed by love.

GLOSSARY

A
abrazos: hugs
abuela: grandmother
agua de pipa: coconut milk
ajolas: Panamanian biscuits
alma: soul
Apúrate!: Hurry up!
arroz con camarones: rice with shrimp
arroz con pollo: rice with chicken
Asi me gustas.: lyrics of a Tito Puente song: "I like it like that; I like you like that."
ay, cariño: oh, honey
Ay, Mamá Inez, todos los negros tomamos café.: words from a folk song: "Mama Inez, all us blacks drink coffee."

B
bacalao: codfish
bachata: a type of Latin American slow-paced guitar music, popular in Panama
¿Baile conmigo?: Will you dance with me?
baile típico: traditional dance
bandolero, bandolero por tu soy: lyrics of a Mariachi song: "Thief, thief, for you I'm…"
barrio: neighborhood
basta: that's enough; stop it
¿Bellísima, no?: Isn't it beautiful?
bellísima: very beautiful
benediciones: prayers
besito: small kiss
besitos: small kisses
besos: kisses
¿Bonita, no?: Isn't it pretty?
boricua: Puerto-Rican

boricua morena: lyrics in the song's chorus: a dark-haired
Puerto-Rican girl
buenas: hi
Bueno.: Hello. (used when answering the phone)
Buenos dias.: Hello.
Buenos dias, Marisolita.: "Good morning, little Marisol."

C

cálmate: calm down
caballero: gentleman; the date of the girl celebrating her quinceañera
caballeros: gentlemen
cafecito: small cup of coffee
campesina: farm girl
capas: party favors; little hats with ribbons attached that say
the quince's name and birthday
carimanoles: fried meat pies made with yucca
cariña: sweetheart; honey
chismes: gossip
claro: of course
claro que sí: of course
como una nativa: like a native
con cariños: with affection
con gusto: with pleasure
con mucha fuerza: with a lot of strength; with a lot of spirit
con sal y limón: with salt and lemon
cuídate: take care
Cuídate. Te amo.: Take care. I love you.
cuídate niña: take care, girl

D

damas: the girls who are part of a quinceañera court
dama de honor: the most important girl in a quinceañera court;
maid of honor
Dame un besito también.: Give me a little kiss, too.
Dame un beso.: Give me a kiss.
Debes ser más tranquila sobre eso.: You should take it easy.

De nada niña.: You're welcome, girl.
de veras: really
Dichosos los ojos!: Great to see you!
discúlpame: excuse me

E
el baile típico: the traditional dance
empanadas: pastry pockets filled with meat
Eres bella.: You look beautiful.
¿Eres loca?: Are you crazy?
Era bellisima.: It was very beautiful.
Es un placer.: It's my pleasure.
Es como nuevo para tí.: It will be like new to you.
Esta buena gente.: They are cool people.
Estoy aqui!: Here I am!
Estoy tarde.: I'm late.
excelente: excellent

F
fabulosa: fabulous
fantasía: costume jewelry
feliz cumpleaños: happy birthday
felicidades: happy birthday
fíjese: listen to this
flores: flowers
fresca: fresh; disrespectful
frijoles negros: black beans
fritura: fritter

G
gracias: thank you
Gracias Abuela.: Thanks, Grandma.
Gracias Tías.: Thanks, Aunts.

H

Hasta la próxima.: See you soon; until the next time I see you.
hija: daughter; also a term of endearment meaning "honey"
Hola.: Hi.
Hola cariño.: Hi, honey.
¿Hola, como estás?: Hi, how are you?
Hola manita: Hi, little sis.
Hola mi amor.: Hi, my love.

I

irascible: an annoying situation

J

jovencita: young girl

K

L

la moda de mami: mommy-style
Las cosas se hacen bien hechas o no se hacen.: Things should be done correctly or not done at all.
las madres: the mothers
Las Meninas: title of a famous painting by Diego Velasquez; literally, the female assistants of the royal court
la patria: the homeland
loca: crazy girl or woman
Los españoles conquistaron con hierro y palabras.: The Spanish conquered with steel and words.
los viejos: the old-time records

M

madrina: godmother
mami: mommy
Mami tenía razón.: Mommy was right.
manita: little sis
mariachi: a Mexican guitar-player and singer

Marisol-Mariposa: Marisol's mother's pet name for her daughter. Mariposa means "butterfly."

mar y sol: sea and sun

mar y cielo: sea and sky

mejor amiga: best friend

Mejor estar sola qué mal acompanado.: Better to be alone than in bad company.

mejores amigas: best friends

mi amiga: my friend

milagritos: small miracle

Mirale!: Check her out!

Mira quién es!: Look who it is!

misa: mass; church service

mojada: wet; soaked

Mucho apura traye cansancio.: Rushing around only makes you tired.

Mucho gusto.: Nice to meet you.

Mundial!: Awesome!

Museo del Barrio: a museum in the Bronx that features Latin-American art

muévete: get moving; hurry up

muy divertido: very fun

N

niña: girl or daughter; also a term of endearment meaning "honey"

No debes planear todo nuestra vida.: You shouldn't plan our whole life.

No debes ser abusadora.: Don't take advantage.

no importa: no big deal

No me digas!: No way!; Don't say that!

No me olvidas.: Don't forget about me.

No seas tan negativa.: Don't be so negative.

No te preocupes: Don't worry about it.

No te preocupes, farolito.: Don't worry about it, honey.

Nosotros te esperamos.: We're waiting for you.

Nosotros vamos a pique.: Our friendship is ending; we're crashing; we're breaking up.

novia: girlfriend

novio: boyfriend

No voy a decirte dos veces!: I'm not going to tell you twice!

O

Oaxaca: a state in southern Mexico

Por supuesto, lo hice yo!: Of course, because I did it!

Olvídale.: Forget about it.

P

padrinos: godparents

papi: daddy

papi chulo: sweet daddy

pasito: a traditional type of dance

patacones: a fried plantains dish

patria: country

Pepito Mala Pata: Dennis the Menace

pernil: roast pork thigh

pero: but

Pero dame un momentito, quiero hablar contigo.: But give me a minute, I want to talk to you.

pero niña…: but, honey…

plátanos: plantains

plátanos maduros: ripe plantains

pobrecito: poor guy

pollera: typical Panamanian folk costume worn for la Pollera, the Panamanian national dance

por favor: please

Por favor, tratas a dar nosotros su atención.: Please, try to give us your attention.

preciosa: honey; beautiful

primo: cousin

Q

¿Que pasa?: What's going on?

¿Qué pasa?: What's up?

Qué placer: What a pleasure.

Qué rompecabezas!: What a headache!

¿Qué tal?: How are you?

¿Qué te pasa?: What's the matter with you?

querida: dear

¿Quién es?: Who is it?

¿Qué piensas?: What do you think?

quince: short for "quinceañera"

quinceañera: a coming-of-age party celebrated on a young woman's 15th birthday.

R

ropa vieja: Cuban meat stew

Recuer das, hija.: You remember, honey.

refrito: refried

S

sabroso: tasty

señorita: miss

si la historia solo fuera como tus manos: if history was only like your hands

Si no él, será otro!: If not him, somebody else!

Somos mejores amigas.: We're best friends.

Soy yo.: It's me.

Son locos.: They're crazy.

Sueños dulces.: Sweet dreams.

T

tamales: stuffed corn cakes

tan suave como su novio, Rubén: as suave as your boyfriend, Ruben

Tarde. Como siempre.: Late. Like always.

Te amo.: I love you.

Te hablo.: I'll talk to you later.

Te hablo mañana.: I'll talk to you tomorrow.
teléfono: telephone
Tenía razón.: He/She was right.
tía/tío: aunt/uncle
tías: aunts
timbales: traditional clothing
Todo es demasiado caro.: Everything is too expensive
tostados de pescado: a fish dish
tranquilo: take it easy
Tú sabes.: You know.

U

un mil gracias: a thousand thanks
una buena charla: a good chat
una comida nacional: a national dish

V

Vámonos!: Let's go!
Vamos por les dulces.: Let's get dessert.
ven: come here
ven acá: come here
venga: come on
Venga a la cocina.: Come into the kitchen.

W

wepa loca: wow!; cool!

X

Y

Ya, basta.: Okay, enough already.
Ya sé.: I already know.
Yo sé.: I know.

Z